THE SWAN BONNET

THE SWAN BONNET

by Katherine L. Holmes

Couchgrass Books

Couchgrass Books
couchgrass-books@centurylink.net

Cover by Paul Beeley, www.create-imaginations.com

Interior photo © Liudmila Gridina I Dreamstime.com

Summary: Swans are endangered in 1920s Alaska. Dawn plans on watching another
migration while in their coastal town, her mother wears a hat to decoy poachers. 1. YA
2. Historical

PROLOGUE

A time ago in the frontier territory, flocks of migrating swans chuffed to the same ocean inlet and swooped down for a night or two in the spring and in the fall. The far bay was hedged in hardy reeds and fenced off by foothills, providing rest and refreshment. Whistler and trumpeter swans arrived as regularly as the mountain streams melted and the snow came. In the spring, one pair stayed to nest while the others flew on. They were waiting in the fall with their cygnets when the swans from the north stopped to strengthen themselves before their journey over the Pacific Ocean.

A few years after 1900, a man came to the inlet with his wife and boy. He built a cabin even if the pair of swans on the bay flaunted their wings at his sailing skiff. They wouldn't be properly introduced until the garden was grown and the woman and boy tossed sunflower seeds along the shore. The man fed them corn when he sailed from the inlet to the waters that were full of salmon.

The new family woke up one autumn morning and found the pair of swans hosting a flotilla of migrators that trampled the shore and feasted on the sunflowers. They ate the last of the corn too but in their wake, the woman found swan feathers and down. She gathered up the precious plumage and took it to the nearest town on the Alaska seacoast. That was half a morning's wagon ride from the cabin under the foothills.

Merchant ships came to the harbor for salmon and fur. The swan feathers sold like caviar.

As more folks moved to Alaska, the family at the bay couldn't help but notice how the migrating flocks were dwindling. Towards 1920, fewer and fewer of the trumpeter swans made rest stops at the inlet. But whistlers still came after nesting in the tundra.

ONE

Hunched at the window frame of her grandfather's cabin, Dawn watched a distressing sight in the vegetable bed. "Grandpa Fen, there's a swan hobbling out there."

She missed the spring migration this year. In previous years, rustling wings like luminous waves greeted her and her father as they approached on the wagon. She was more than 14-years-old but her father still wouldn't let her ride a horse out to the inlet.

Because the traveling swans were gone already, Grandpa Fen regaled Dawn with the story he told since she first saw a migration. He was careful not to talk about the swans in town and she was too, even if the swans had already made their stopover for the season. Summers, she could still see the resident pair, Bustle and Sir Swan, as they raised their cygnets. And since she was ten, a second pair stayed at the inlet. Her grandmother named them Pinion and Minion.

"I was getting to that," Grandpa Fen said. "It's Bustle, the old swan. Older in her lifespan than I am. Sir Swan, he didn't come back this spring." Grandpa Fen's hair was silvering like the streaks on the salmon he hauled in.

"Sir Swan didn't come back?" Dawn started.

Grandma Glenda answered, "That's probably made Bustle forlorn." She handed Dawn a sack of grain and then she eased the cabin door open. Outside, they scattered the feed for Bustle and then they sprinkled more along the shore for Pinion and Minion.

"More migrators might come," Dawn hoped. "Maybe Sir Swan, too."

Dawn's father, Young Fen, was coming from the barn where he had refreshed the horses. He paused when he saw the old swan stretching her neck for the grain. Then he crouched down to examine Bustle. After she elbowed him with her wing, he shook his head. "Yep, it must be Bustle. I've never seen her like this, not even after a tussle with the younger pair. Usually, she'd flap both her wings at me and drive me off. See if she's afeard of Dawn."

Dawn crept near but as she did, the swan shambled towards the water. Sidling near her, Dawn couldn't help but stroke the flounce of Bustle's wings. They were like something spun and for the first time, Bustle hadn't flapped her into retreat. Even though Dawn had seen catalog drawings of satin dresses, she had never seen a fabric so glistening.

"Maybe Sir Swan was detained by weather," Dawn said, standing back in case Bustle wanted to feed near the shore.

"He always flies in about the time she does," her father said. "Your grandma heard gunshot, right after the migrators landed. That's how we didn't get out here in time."

"It scared them all off?" Her grandfather ran into hunters on his land but Dawn hadn't heard him complain much about swan poaching. He didn't mind bear hunting near his cabin if he knew the men. Before Dawn was born though, her grandparents had to stop poachers from trespassing during the swan migrations. Then in 1918, when she was just four, a law in the states made swan hunting illegal.

"They were scared up," Grandma Glenda said. "Fen was gone fishing."

"I guess I know why they'd dare to come here," said Young Fen. "There were two of us when I was young and when swan hunting wasn't illegal. Seems like someone knew Pa was out fishing."

"Three of us," Glenda said. "I guess we got used to things being quiet. It's hard for Fen to stay back from the spring salmon."

"Had to remind people that they were on our property," Dawn's father said to her. "People round here know well enough. Well, I guess I need some coffee."

Dawn and Grandma Glenda stayed outside to admire Bustle. It had to be her because she remained at the shore with the three of them talking. She had found the trail of feed and was huddled near the reeds. Her feathers showed no age.

"She might still be frightened from the gunshot," Glenda said. "And she's wary of the younger pair."

Pinion and Minion still floated out on the bay like huge water lilies.

"When Pinion and Minion came in 1924, oh, the flapping and ferocity that went on! Then the two pairs plodded to opposite sides of the lake like Irishmen building in the bog. Well, Bustle made for her old spot. But she must have been lonely there."

Dawn followed her grandmother's gaze across the shoreline to the north side of the bay. "What if Sir Swan was killed?"

"There might have been forty swans landed yesterday."

"Bustle was fine last year. Maybe she's just scared."

"She tried to accompany Minion over to her nesting site but Pinion drove her off." They ventured closer but Bustle's billowy wing tottered. Glenda stepped back. "She might be tired from her long flying this spring. Seems weak as a fawn."

"She wasn't this tired last year," Dawn said.

Dawn and her grandmother went back into the cabin. There, Grandpa Fen told another tale, one that reminded Dawn of an old knit comforter, re-yarned in places. It was of hardship and fortune, about how her grandparents left Ireland and voyaged to the Alaska territory for a pot of gold. This was her father's favorite account since he knew the swans as a boy. Dawn sat near the window, keeping an eye on Bustle, as Grandpa Fen recalled.

In Ireland, the country doctor told Glenda that she might never have children. She was already twenty-three-years-old and when she lost a child, she felt as empty as a woman past child-bearing. Yet before that, she was as hardy as a horse. Nevertheless, she could be persuaded to venture with Fen to America and, because no one was hanging on her skirts, she was ready to take a prairie schooner west. It wasn't just the search for a place like Ireland. The gold fever had taken hold of both her and Fen. Glenda was willing to become one of the few women panning for the treasure. They'd planned on traveling to California but when they heard about the gold in Alaska, they went there instead of crossing the American desert.

By the time Fen was rattling up his leprechaun's share of gold, crouched on a river bank, Glenda was sitting with Young Fen. He liked playing with the sand in her pan. The prospecting became unprofitable, shared with herds of like-minded individuals lining the rivers as though they were parched. But eventually, the nuggets coming downstream were ice.

That started Glenda's old yearning for a climate like Ireland. But such a climate wasn't very far south. The leprechaun's pot was easily transported and parted with for the cabin acreage south of Fairbanks, almost on the ocean coast of Alaska. There the waters burnished with salmon in the springtime. No sooner had Fen found that salmon could be picked from the water like poppies in a breeze than the swans flew in, their wings spread like angels. When Young Fen was old enough to ask about the leprechaun's pot, it had vanished in that land under the mountains.

"And now they say a man with a white parachute can fly down from an airplane like a swan," Grandpa Fen said, turning the pages of a San Francisco newspaper that Dawn's father brought him. Its 1928 news was weeks old.

TWO

Grandpa Fen didn't say exactly what happened to the old swan, Bustle. Although Dawn saw her again, a yarn circulated about her demise. And if that yarn was knitted up, Grandpa Fen wasn't one to be caught wearing his sweater inside-out.

Towards July, he noticed that the old swan wasn't bobbing along near Pinion and Minion as she had managed to do since their four cygnets started swimming. When he sailed in from fishing, looking over the snowcap reflections for the swans, he didn't see Bustle until he was almost to shore. She was becoming anchored in the reeds and sometimes when Fen didn't see her at all and feared the worst, he found her hunkered in the garden. If Fen bent down to touch her, she winced more than she repelled him. Glenda came out, calling "Bustle!" the way she used to when the swans stamped in the green corn shoots. But now it was to scatter more feed for her.

When Dawn came to keep Glenda company, what she did every summer for a week at a time, Glenda was making Bustle a pet.

"She's gotten her strength back," Dawn observed. Yet she wondered at Glenda for making Bustle a part of her barnyard where chickens, the cow, and Wallop the horse grazed. The old swan's wings were still grand, especially when she swiped at a chicken that interrupted her along the trail of currants that Glenda scattered. And she was getting used to Dawn's presence as she sat on the cabin stoop, learning the stitches for fishermen knit sweaters.

In a breeze-blown voice, Glenda related memories about Bustle as if the swan could comprehend her. Of course, Dawn's father wanted to make a pet of her when he was a boy. Young Fen thought Bustle might walk along with him like the dog. Little did he expect that he would get a feisty punch from a wing. Bustle and Sir Swan taught him to take his punches and to know when he might get beat.

"There he was, thrown to the ground, and often it was muddy." Glenda pointed her knitting needle at the shoreline. "Why, he learned what whitecaps are out there on the cold sea, being around those swans when he wasn't four feet high."

Glenda had collected a number of feathers from Bustle over the summer. "Never so many from one swan," she said one night, letting Dawn pick out a feather for a drawing pen. Then Grandpa Fen honed its tip and required her to write to Reynolds at the General Store about the price Glenda wanted for her eggs, butter, and the berries that were ripening on the foothill. Dawn's father practiced his letters with a swan plume when he was young. He could only get to school when Grandpa Fen was fishing, taking the skiff there, or when Glenda drove to town. In fact, they all practiced in the evening with the schoolbooks.

Dawn would rather draw with the plume than learn Glenda's knitting stitches. If she drew Bustle, her grandmother was content to tell another story about her.

"I don't suppose Alex Tuskoffey told you about Bustle and the grizzly. The grizzly that gave us the rug inside."

"Maybe he did." Dawn's uncle was in the north hunting but he usually stayed with them about the time the autumn ships came.

"He said he'd track the grizzly that eluded Fen. The cow wouldn't give any milk, she was so frightened, and there were a few chickens less. When Alex came with his dog, Bustle floated away from her cygnets, off to the north shore over there where a spring stream is hidden. Well, that's where Alex found the bear tracks."

"He says hunters use other animals for tracking."

"He believed she sensed something about him. But when Alex met Bustle at the shore after bringing in that grizzly, she doused his face! I suppose she knew about his gun and attempted to distract him from her cygnets."

"Leading him to the grizzly?"

"It makes a person wonder. After that, he never bothered to hunt on the side of the bay near the cygnets. He even says that his traps did better on the opposite side, up there near the bottleneck."

However Dawn drew the old swan on paper, it was Bustle's eye that centered the lines. This saddened Dawn so that when she had the opportunity to feed Minion and Pinion, she stayed at the shore for as long as they visited for their easy grain. Minion made her dance, doffing a wing in a warning way and catching at the apron Dawn wore over her skirt and boots when she stayed with Glenda.

One cloudy afternoon, Minion veered with her cygnets towards shore. Grandpa Fen's skiff came in, its sails like huge wingspreads, and sometimes he fed them leftover bread from his lunch. Dawn helped him with his catch and then went back to the water's edge where she could watch the cygnets chasing one another.

Afraid that she was preventing Bustle from joining them, she sat at the bench near the door. There she heard Fen arguing with Glenda.

"You've been leaving the door open! Ta invite a wolverine to dinner?"

"Dawn's out there."

"Down at the shore!"

"The old swan wanders so near that she might come in."

"That swan doesn't know where she is! She's let *me* touch her. She won't make it to any California seashore this fall."

"She's becoming tame, like a farmyard goose."

"She's not getting around like a farmyard goose. Do you think she'll live in a barn, feral as she is?"

Dawn watched Bustle tipping down the slope towards the other swans.

"What are you getting at, Fen? Your voice has the sound of gold fever in it. As if you'd heard a rumor about a vein of gold."

"Pannin' up north caused me to note a being's constitution. The old swan isn't breathing right in that long neck of hers."

"She's huffing at you."

"She used to attack. Glenda, I can't help but think that she's spared that journey south."

"I'm fixing to take care of her."

"How are you going to do that? Net her when she tries to fly? If I was so old and bereaved but still had the strength to fell a tree, I'd a' soon that if a tree was contrary, it hit me hard rather than languish. There are some nets, and here's one, that are past mending."

"They say that swans are seldom sick and that an animal's hardy enough if it's eating. Well, the raspberries on the hill are starting to ripen and Reynolds is going to expect some or they'll think we're making wine. Dawn and I can go see about them before we go back into town."

"As if you couldn't spend all of August harvesting berries for wine."

Sometimes Dawn suspected that her grandfather was becoming hard of hearing, he talked so loudly. She walked down to the shore again where Bustle was settled in the water now and gliding as if she were one of the cygnets. On the dock where the boat was tied, Dawn watched the first drops of rain land on the old swan's cloud of feathers.

~~~

After Glenda brought Dawn back to town, the argument about Bustle spurted as frequently as coffee did from the spout. The old swan dozed in the garden when she'd had her fill of greens, just where Glenda could keep an eye on her. But when Fen came back from fishing, Bustle moved as if her feet were anchors, doddering down to the reeds.

"She might be resting to gain strength," Glenda said.

"Even if she's sunflower-fed, it's awful to think of her old wings attempting the long flight," Fen replied. "She'll probably land anywhere from sheer weakness. Her feathers will get gnashed by vermin. She'd give a wolf milk whiskers. Do you know what Alex Tuskoffey would pay for a swanskin? I'm not sure myself but it'd be plenty for the catalog china you've been admirin'. Enough for me to have a safer sailboat."

"People would think we were poaching swans! We're not starving the way we were in '06. It's poaching even if they're not reminding people of that in town. They figure everyone remembers the 1918 Act when the new folks can say they didn't know. Why would anyone think they could purchase a swanskin here? It's as illegal here as it is in the States."

"The fact is it's talked of. That swan won't survive another year and it's a special case." Fen was stubborn. "It's not swan hunting at all. Right now, the sheriff's got so much trouble with tinhorns coming into town that he wouldn't accuse us. It sure wouldn't look good though, if I brought a swanskin into town around the time of the fall migration. That swan won't fly out with the others. You'd feel awful bad if she tried."

Fen spread out a fishing net until he could see a shredded place. He muttered, "I'm only sayin' that to the fur companies, a swanskin is worth a horse right now. And we could sure use a good horse, speaking of aging animals. You keep complaining about Wallop when that swan is on its last flight feathers. Young Fen said that too."

"And you think Alex Tuskoffey will smuggle it for you."

"It'd be just a pelt to him. And nothing but a secret to some of the traders he's encountered. Why if he was here today, he'd say there's a natural law that you can't fight with, Glenda. And maybe you're keeping that swan close so you can pluck its feathers."

THREE

One afternoon, Glenda left Bustle near the reeds and climbed into the foothills to gather raspberries and salmonberries. She was so miffed at Fen that she stayed there when she saw his skiff glide into the bottleneck of the inlet. She hovered near the soggy thicket where the raspberries grew, feeling remiss. Fen favored them. He hadn't netted his usual catch this summer and even though he signed onto a larger salmon boat, he said that the younger men were snatching up more than their share.

Spotting some cloudberries, Glenda remembered how Bustle loved them. She used to poise herself, ready to flaunt her wings, if Glenda gave her a handful. Now she would probably never find them on the bank near her nesting site again. And maybe she last saw her other love, Sir Swan, at the bay.

Glenda surveyed the valley, guessing where the gunshot came during the spring migration. By the time she saw Fen docking his boat, she had forgotten their squabble. She made her way down the slope but she couldn't help but cull the berries she saw amongst the blue lupines. The bushes made a zigzag trail, easier for her to follow than the steep creek that flowed towards their cabin. She was thinking how a bear would be disappointed at the picked-over bushes when she heard a dull cracking sound that sent a shiver of uneasiness through her.

The noise might have been a bucket banging against an oarlock or a tool resonating on a rock. But she heard a rippling sound in the ravine, like a faint brogue. The cracking noise was most probably a gun. In all her years at the bay, Glenda had never heard a swansong.

With a gasp, Glenda gathered up her berry baskets. She clambered down the foothill but as she reached the clearing of her cottage, she steadied her gait. She saw that Fen was standing over Bustle. He had shot her.

"I found that swan in a swoon. She was on her way to the sunflowers," Fen said. "I couldn't stand it any longer."

"You must be fooling me. She was strong enough to cry out a swansong."

"She had a strong spirit. Surprised me too," Fen said in a hush. He gritted his teeth as he prepared to convey Bustle's carcass to the barn.

Glenda looked out at Pinion and Minion, far across the lake with their new cygnets. "Your gun scares the swans as much as a poacher's gun."

"They're feeding over there. The young swans haven't shown Bustle any notice for weeks. Look, her feathers are still thick. Her body is shrunken. At least this splendid pelt didn't sink into the mud or became a wolf's milk whiskers."

Glenda couldn't help Fen bring the old swan to the barn.

FOUR

To Glenda's vexation, Fen hung the swanskin on a rope he tacked up in their cottage. While the hide dried, the feathers fluttered and glistened. But they were anything but morbid.

Glenda no longer thought of Bustle as a sick old swan. She found herself musing on past delights in her life: cloudberries under dusty ferns, cradle linings arranged like petals, snowflakes that landed on her sleeve and vanished.

The swan feathers were in her peripheral view but instead of paining her, they gave her the sensation that she was close to a cloud. Many years before, when shooting swans was legal in the Alaskan territory, she winced at seeing a swanskin, at a swan being destroyed for its feathers. She could collect feathers fallen from swans and sell them for hat plumes.

On market day, Glenda set out the few plumes that the resident swans shed near her cabin. She wiped their stalks, once to clean off the dirt and again with oil to protect them. Then she packed the plumes in a muslin coverlet and plumped the swan's down into a muslin pouch. It was with the quickness of her hopeful youth that she did these tasks. She felt less slap-dashed than usual with the swanskin like a shaft of calm in her cabin.

How had Glenda become so rugged about everything? She wondered as she sharpened the ends of two perfect plumes. Why did she haul the cow around instead of patting it? She forgot to complain to Fen about the ferocious, stingy men that she dealt with in the harbor town. But she didn't ask him as he sat by the oil lamp why she had become rugged.

"I've plucked a feather of Bustle's," Glenda said. "It's a memento of her. And the other's a drawing pen for Dawn. To think that swan feathers were in demand as ink pens are now. I can't think of much need for swan feathers now except mummery."

"Still, a swanskin would get a price from some of those ship merchants," Fen replied. He was reading another San Francisco newspaper, passed to him from a fishing mate. "You can send for those dishes you've been wanting. Old Sir Swan's swanskin must be trodden to mud somewhere."

"If he wasn't poached," Glenda reminded him.

Fen grimaced at Glenda. "Young Fen and me will be watching during the fall migration. He's talking to Sheriff Farefax about it. There's likely poaching where no one's watching these days. If you'd like, I'll go to town tomorrow. We'll just sell the swanskin to Alex Tuskoffey. Heard he's come and was down at the harbor today."

"No, not when Alex pulls that nugget of gold from his pocket. You'll come back with fool's eyes and mouth to match, all a garble about going up to Nome. Now, what if someone accuses us of poaching?"

"Tell them the truth," Grandpa Fen said, laying down his newspaper. "The old swan was so frail that she couldn't get from the lake to the corn. And then she collapsed. Sheriff Farefax'll know that if I was so greedy, I'd have shot that swan in '17, the year before the Act made it illegal."

"Maybe I'm getting greedy for a swan pelt now. I could make a featherbed out of it."

"What if someone looked in the featherbed for hidden liquor?" Grandpa Fen took up his newspaper again and turned towards the lamp. "Besides, that would be sleeping like a lord. I don't know how I'd get up to go salmon fishing."

"Easier than me going to market tomorrow," Glenda said.

"Then I'll take it all in on the skiff this time. You sell things too quickly to Tuskoffey. As soon as his talk gets gruesome and he has you seein' his toes frostbit and near being amputated, you stop bargaining. You didn't get the going price for the red fox I shot."

"And if you went to town, you'd be over to Toddy's and thinking you'd seen a leprechaun so prosperous that he'd gotten his wishes. And mighty as Finn MacCool, he knew of some creek where you won't find pots of gold and copper and God knows what."

Fen got up and strolled to the swanskin. As he clasped it to check its hide, feathers flipped into his face, causing him to sneeze and cough.

He stepped back from it, inhaling, and after he took out his pocket handkerchief, he dabbed at an eye. "Might as well get it to market tomorrow," he said. "There's a ship in the harbor."

~~~

When she prepared for market, Glenda usually braced herself for the coarse and cursing men in the harbor town. She loaded her wagon with butter, eggs, and salmon. And then there were the berries, a special basket for her stop at Young Fen's house. This was like other market days except that she would have to tell Dawn and her mother, Petra, as much as she could about Bustle.

It was gone, the last glistening stay of the swan Glenda fed for so many years. First she wrapped Bustle's swanskin in muslin, and then she put it in a burlap bag. As she carried it out of the cabin, she could feel the grizzly rug grazing her ankles. It made her feel roughhewn and reckless again.

Once, she felt lithe as a Sitka black-tailed deer. But life in Alaska demanded that her movements be more moose-like than deer-like. *How could she be otherwise with the trouncing wind and the treacherous terrain to contend with?* Glenda wondered. She had to slap Wallop with the reins because the mottled horse wanted to alter their trail again. They sauntered along a route bordered with blue hare's-tail grass and littered rocks. Fen allowed Wallop to forge this roundabout way instead of panting on the steeper road that he took when he was a young horse.

Now they risked grizzlies. Fen saw more bears clawing up salmon at the shore than Glenda had ever seen. Even if Wallop could gallop faster on the low trail, it made Glenda nervous if he plunged too near the trees. The grizzly might go for the salmon while Glenda jumped on Wallop and rode like the wind. She had only been so scared once, afraid that the grizzly might not get to the salmon and attack her instead. Since, she thought it would be best to shoot a grizzly from the wagon seat.

"You wild, plodding rascal!" she couldn't help but yell. "You're wading a third trail!"

Glenda's voice still had an Irish lilt to it but her whiplash didn't have the edge that Fen's had. Still, she would rather put up with the seemingly deaf horse than have Fen talk about touchstones and gold dust. After selling his salmon, he might take a dinghy up some inconsequential stream, put out a salmon net while he panned for gold, stare at rainbows in the rapids, and return with a measly catch. Glenda had done the marketing since before Prohibition because Fen used to get tied up at Toddy's saloon.

But a man with a recurring desire to fish up metal from a river was much better company than whatever she saw on the road ahead. It looked like a bear cub, worse thing. As they reached the animal, Wallop lurched and Glenda grabbed her shotgun from the wagon seat, just in time to see the tail of a wolverine. She almost fired except that the shotgun barrel caught the boot string tied around the swan parcel. She had pulled up the bundle but now it was undone and feathers splayed out. They spread over Glenda's hand as she put the pelt back on the wagon, tied it, and let Wallop forge his third trail.

Setting the shotgun over the parcel, Glenda thought of bear cubs. If her eyes hadn't seen right and it was a bear cub, her shot might have made the trip back truly fearful. On his cleared trail again, Wallop was galloping steadily so that Glenda could consider her bitter bouts in the wagon. Bears were the only animals that could possibly overcome her unless a desperate man held her up. She considered Bustle and the years that her eggs produced cygnets, how she somehow fooled the wolverine and maintained her statue-like calm.

"Wallop, I guess you can sense what's in those trees," she said, letting the rein out on the old horse. The trail whizzed beneath her.

FIVE

At her father's smokehouse, Dawn had to wipe a window on the street in order to see Wallop, the headstrong horse, clopping into town. She wondered if the four cygnets were flying yet and how Bustle was.

In August, their small port brought in people from Juneau and Seattle, and people on their way to Anchorage where the mud flats made the navigation more difficult. That brought a high demand for smoked salmon.

When her father was too busy to ride or take a sailing boat to her grandparents', Dawn suggested that she might accompany Grandma Glenda home on horseback. But then she'd have to ride back to town alone since there was always some needlework at home. Grandma Glenda had been driving a wagon alone ever since Young Fen could remember.

Young Fen wouldn't even allow Dawn to stand at the door of the smokehouse where folks were more likely to pass the time of day than to buy the salmon inside. Even the fishermen he knew had taken to teasing Dawn.

"Grandma's come in," she called into the hazy air of the building.

"We'll help her with them crates," Young Fen said, marking a ledger near the smoke chamber. The Aleut man, Jon, could attend the smokehouse when her father wasn't there.

But Glenda was taking a burlap bag from the front seat of the wagon. She took it around to the back and put it between the crates of cleaned salmon.

"She might have a fur for Uncle Alex," Dawn said.

Her father pulled on his caribou hide jacket as Dawn went out to tie a feedbag on Wallop. The noise on the street, sailors talking to men in lumberjack jackets, muffled Dawn's greeting. Her grandmother was occupied with the crates of fish when Young Fen came out, rubbing his mutton chops.

"Did you see Alex? He was down at the harbor," he said to Dawn.

"Not yet. He said if he gets his price for fur, he's staying long enough to build us a winter sledge." She surveyed the harbor across the road, hoping to see her uncle sally over in his sealskin jacket and summer boots. The other night, he came back from the north, loaded with furs.

"Your uncle says a lot of things. Doesn't Alex say a lot of things, Ma? Dawn shouldn't get him goin' on his snow ghosts and tirades of ice. There's a few too many polar bears in the brigades he's seen near Nome. Your grandpa and I have been north, Dawn. Some are sensible and don't tell of treks too long and too cold for the newcomers.   What have you brought here, Ma?"

Her father nearly made her trot, grasping her arm so that she would move from the boardwalk. She was bareheaded and wearing her new gray flannel jacket, sewn with the same pattern as her hide jacket. Since the springtime, a ship was usually in the harbor. Along with the newcomer prospectors, a few strange men had tweaked a long braid from behind. Frances at the Snow Clothing store observed that her gray flannel brought out the reddish strands of her hair. Dawn usually spent her time in town at the Snow Clothing store where her mother might pass the time with Frances, sewing fur boots and mittens.

Today though, her father was hunkered over the wagon so she couldn't see if Grandma Glenda brought a fur. The fact was, Uncle Alex would probably pay more for it than Frances would at Snow Clothing. There he was, swaggering from the Snow Clothing store down the street. Frances had sewn a secret pocket in Uncle Alex's sealskin jacket. He kept a big nugget of gold there and when he showed it, there weren't any men interested in braids. Alex Tuskoffey could draw a crowd, telling how his father found the nugget near Fairbanks just before the gold rush, and then he laughed with a swipe of his hand. He had hung onto it even though the gold rush happened thirty years ago.

Uncle Alex usually added to some that he couldn't have afforded to keep his nugget if he spent his time prospecting for gold. When a fray turned into a fracas, he might describe where exactly the nugget was found.   Then he routed the roustabouts to a place that was already excavated.

Patting Wallop's flank, Dawn saw a small swan feather on the wagon seat. She retrieved it and took it to her grandmother as her father hoisted a crate of salmon. "Is Bustle still weakened?" she asked.

Her grandmother handed her a smaller parcel from the bag, long as a ruler, another feather for a drawing pen. "She could climb the shore to the feed. Keep this one. For your best letters." The pockets of Glenda's cheeks were low on her face. She looked like that when she talked of Ireland, but now she was staring at the burlap bag.

"Uncle Alex says that writing with a feather is for cravens. He says I should get paints and draw with a pencil."

"Swan plumes don't come off a craven bird. Well, Alex doesn't mind providing ivory for those carvers and their fancy scrimshaw."

"Dawn," her father said at her shoulder. "You might take the eggs and butter over to the General Store."

"For Grandma?" Dawn turned towards Glenda. "Aren't you going in for flour, Grandma?"

"She's lookin' for your Uncle Alex right now."

"Did Grandpa Fen get an otter?" Dawn asked, eyeing the bundle.

"Bustle wasn't strong enough to get from the garden to the shore one day," Grandma Glenda said in her forthright way. "Her swanskin is in this parcel."

Dawn stared at the burlap that contained the swan feathers she could hardly stroke.

Young Fen looked around and said, "I didn't think Bustle could make another migration. We could take it to the smokehouse but Jon is working in there."

"We could drive to your house," Glenda said. "But I want to talk with Alex myself. No, Bustle couldn't get around any better after you last saw her, Dawn."

Dawn stayed near the bundle while her father and Glenda unloaded the fish. She could feel the springy feathers, what would look like spilt milk to her mother. Dawn hadn't ever seen a swan pelt before. She was almost relieved to see her Uncle Alex slogging towards them in his sealskin. He would put the beautiful remains on a ship. Bustle's pelt would be made into sprays for hats and headpieces. Or it would be plucked for powder puffs and pillows. Ladies would make use of it in temperate climates, catalog ladies.

~~~

As Uncle Alex approached, Dawn's greeting didn't climb from her throat to her lips. She thought about how the swan pelt would be like a King Salmon in the smokehouse to him.

"Alex Tuskoffey! You must float on those boots of yours," Glenda said, allowing Uncle Alex to extend a sly hand towards the mouth of the burlap bag. Even though he was smiling, his glossy black mustache made a daunting scowl and then he pulled the bag open so he could look into it. "You have a swan pelt!" he murmured.

"I have a few feathers and some swan's down for you." Glenda's voice could lilt like a feather.

"Better that I take it all than you selling it at the store over there. Frances doesn't usually sell to the ships." Uncle Alex lowered his voice. "You wouldn't know the worth of a swanskin in the last years, I guess."

Glenda retorted, "She was worth at least eighty cygnets in her time, Alex."

"It's the old nesting swan!" Dawn's voice had overcome the steep part of her throat. She looked around to see if anyone heard even though the boots on the boardwalk made enough noise.

"I thought I'd bring it to Frances when I take my knitting to Snow Clothing," Glenda said. "Those ship people buy fur from her counter often enough."

"She won't sell this to them. What would she do with it?" Uncle Alex objected.

Glenda answered, "There's plenty of women around here who'd like the feathers for their hats. Frances can pluck it."

Young Fen was back and he said, "It's awfully fine for the use of some of them. Even if there's occasion for the women to wear feathers in their hats."

"Frances won't pay what I've heard quoted." Uncle Alex was spreading the feathers on his hand under the burlap, hands that were scabrous from snow and ice. "Not for pluckin' to fill a comforter. Or to make some adornment that might be sported in a Fairbanks saloon. When they serve their cider."

Young Fen put a hand on the bundle. "What I'd like to know, Alex, is why anyone would quote you the price of this pelt?"

"Because this is only a territory. Because they think I have the name of a lawless Russian. Because they think I have native blood. Probably 'cause I know my way around." Uncle Alex's mustache drooped more scowlishly when he wasn't smiling. He never gave Dawn's father explanations as if he owed any. His grandfather, Dawn's great-grandfather, came to the Alaska territory when the Russians ruled it, years before Fen and Glenda came from Ireland. And Uncle Alex, like her mother, also had native Aleut blood.

"We were fixing to take it to the house. But four's a crowd on the wagon," Young Fen said.

Alex stared Young Fen in the face. "Easier to take it from here to the harbor. Especially if someone shot it."

This made Dawn flinch while Glenda stood motionless as a wooden baluster on the boardwalk. "That beauty was more than twenty years old, Alex," she said. "She was feeble and her mate didn't migrate back this spring. Why, she collapsed when she was feeding on shore. You know we haven't been shooting swans to sell them! It was illegal to shoot swans in Britain, for centuries it was. I don't care if I have to tell the sheriff about it."

"Her mate might have been poached," Young Fen said. "She was floating on the bay alone." He turned towards the boardwalk so that Uncle Alex looked that way too. The deputy sheriff and Davy, his son, had just come out of Thaddeus's Hotel and Eatery. "I know the sheriff hasn't had time to chase swan poachers. And the liquor prohibition keeps the deputy busy." Young Fen nodded towards the deputy even though he was yards away. "Dawn, you might take those eggs and butter over to the General Store. See if Davy needs anything for his mother first. They're always waitin' for the berries."

As Dawn found the crate with the crock of butter and the basket of eggs, her father continued. "My mother thinks there's been poaching near the cabin. You might have an idea who it is, Alex, hearing those quotes from people."

"You hear them talkin' all the time over at Toddy's when the ships anchor. I guess you don't eat supper there much." Uncle Alex laughed with as much bluff as he had with a hunting partner. "In this territory, the snow is Czar, the ice is King, and the President is a berg floating offshore."

"And there's the deputy," Young Fen said as Glenda put one of her berry baskets in the crate. "He's talking to one of those ship people." He stopped Dawn with his eyebrows. "What have you heard them quote at Toddy's exactly?" Young Fen motioned for Uncle Alex to confer nearer Wallop as if the horse could help them arrive at a price.

"The natural demise of that bird is not an exactly, it's a haggling." Uncle Alex strode towards Young Fen, who said sharply, "Dawn! The eggs!"

She turned to see Davy coming down the boardwalk ahead of his father. He had his new elk hide hat on and his eyes, seeing Uncle Alex, were as sharp as Deputy Shamison's badge. Davy was more interested in accompanying his father and his aims than anything else. Everyone at school knew it. Dawn stepped up to the boardwalk as Davy reached the smokehouse.

"Davy! My grandma brought some berries."

"She did." Davy wasn't the kind of boy to tweak braids.

"I've got to take them to the store. Is that where you're headed?" Davy knew that Young Fen didn't like Dawn walking on her own.

"I guess we're not stopping for any salmon," Davy replied.

Young Fen stretched a mutton chop towards Deputy Shamison while Uncle Alex turned towards the harbor, crossing his arms.

Dawn said, "Uncle Alex just came. I guess my dad wants to know his plans."

Behind them, Deputy Shamison shouted, "How long you gonna be in town, Alex?"

"At least until the next ship arrives," Uncle Alex returned.

"Says he's going to build us a sledge," Young Fen said by way of humor.

Since Uncle Alex wasn't talking to any new folks, the deputy caught up with Davy.

"She's brought some berries in," Davy said. "I wonder who's gonna buy them."

"Could be someone aimin' to make wine," his father replied.

The two strode with Dawn, probably to keep an eye on the berries and to ask Mr. Reynolds who else wanted them. Once Dawn collected what her grandmother required from Mr. Reynolds, she was relieved that Davy had no obligation to walk her back to the wagon.

SIX

On the store verandah, Dawn saw that her father and Uncle Alex were still at their haggling. But by the time she reached Grandma Glenda, Young Fen stood over the burlap bag, his back to the boardwalk. His words were nearly overwhelmed by the rumbling of wagon wheels and a ship's horn.

"No Ma, I'll buy it for what Alex said he'd pay."

"I don't want you to do that, Young Fen."

Dawn listened, hoping that her father would buy Bustle's swanskin. But Uncle Alex protested, "I thought he was bargaining for you, Glenda! You'll let me pay what I will. What do you want with this pelt? Who do you know on the ship from Frisco, Young Fen?"

"I'm giving it to Petra on her birthday," Young Fen muttered but when he saw Dawn, his mutton chops twitched. "Well, I thought I'd surprise you too, Dawn."

"Petra! What does my sister want with it?"

"Alex, if my son wants something I bring into town, I can't sell it to you." If Glenda's voice lilted like a feather, it had firmed on the wing. "I'd prefer that those merchants didn't think there were any such pelts for the selling here."

Uncle Alex glared. Glenda knew he didn't care what people thought of him. He often brought wild stories from the north along with the furs he proffered.

Astonished at her father this time, Dawn watched the swan pelt being transacted. She couldn't imagine her mother making finery of it, what she'd seen in catalogs. Her mother stitched boots out of fur and skin. She wove braiding for parkas. The only feathers she used were small ones sewn in a native pattern she learned from her mother. Since Petra hardly ever went to the inlet, she wouldn't think about Bustle when she saw the pelt.

~~~

Passing on the boardwalk amongst the men in mackintoshes and hide jackets were a few women in shirtwaists and felt-brimmed hats. Everyone wore water-stained boots. The unfamiliar women, whether they came on a ship or were those associated with men at Toddy's when the supper tables were used for cards, would be as excited to see the swan pelt as if it were sugar frosting, a scrimshaw tusk, or the Northern lights.

Dawn mused, "I wonder if Ma would make a featherbed out of it." Her mother might want to hide the feathers in the way that Uncle Alex hid his gold nugget.

"She'd have to fill it with goose feathers too," her father answered. "I thought I'd ask Frances to make something from it. Something like a new hat. Dawn, promise you won't say a word about it to Petra."

Dawn nodded her head and looked at a cloud pluming over the ocean. A swan pelt at their house was so perplexing an idea that she wouldn't know how to introduce it anyway.

Glenda said in a whisper, "In Ireland, a hat with swan feathers is like you, Alex, with your nugget of gold."

"My sister wearing swan on her head? She's not used to wearing sprays in her hats." Uncle Alex was outraged. "Native women would laugh at her. Folks here would wonder at her. She'll probably pluck it like you could, Glenda. When people in the States are deprived of swan feathers."

"Swan would keep a woman's head as dry as fur in the rainy weather," Young Fen surmised. "She's worn a swan feather in the summertime. You know yourself, Alex, that beaver hunting isn't what it was because all the beaver over here went to hats in Europe. Russia too."

"Russia first. Beaver hats!" Uncle Alex sneered.

But Uncle Alex brought them polar bear fur for hats. The town was used to seeing Dawn and her mother wearing white fur in the winter. She protested, "What's the difference between a swan hat and a polar bear hat for winter? I guess nobody in the States can get polar bear fur there."

"The folks in this town know that I ambushed polar bears to get that fur. Them bears basking on the snow and ready for a fight," Uncle Alex boasted. "What does a swan hat tell you?"

"That's exactly it," Young Fen said. "I'm not selling it. Petra can use the down and smaller feathers for her Aleut pattern."

"Petra in a swan hat!" Uncle Alex guffawed. And then he strode towards the harbor.

The jutting whiskers on Young Fen's face hid his smile lines. He looked hard at Dawn. "If you don't tell your mother about the swan pelt, she'll give Frances advice when she's at the store. She might even help her work with the swanskin. Then she'll be pleased with her birthday present, despite what Alex thinks."

"What if he tells her? He'll probably be over tonight," Dawn said.

"I don't think he's going to want to talk about it. He probably doesn't believe that I'd give it to Petra."

Glenda put Bustle's bundle in Young Fen's arms and her tone was serious. "I wonder if someone from around here was responsible for that gunshot last spring. Alex and Frances's father don't hunt when the swans migrate. They just check their traps. I don't want to hear another gun this fall."

She knew Dawn would never announce the swan migration to anyone. In the spring though, Davy Shamison had stopped by their house at dusk. That was unusual and what was more unusual was that Davy sat with her on the front door stoop where she was watching the sky. He said he'd had trouble with a grammar assignment at school but then he tricked her into showing him her drawings inside the house. On top was a drawing of swans in their vector, one line of migrators higher than the other as seen from below. She'd been vexed at the wingspreads, expecting a swan plume to help her drawing. Only a few times had she seen swans flying over the darkened ocean. Davy said he'd never seen a totem pole with one swan above another. When she tried to turn the subject to another drawing, a puffin, Davy asked her about the swan migration. All she answered was that her swan plume needed sharpening. Swan plumes were magical in her drawing hand but Davy scoffed at the use of them like Uncle Alex did.

"You go on to the Snow Clothing Store with Grandma, Dawn," her father directed her. "When I see the wagon gone, I'll bring the swan pelt over there."

Dawn watched him carrying the bundle around to the back door of the smokehouse. The parcel took up his forearms and he handled it as if it were much more valuable than a fur. She couldn't be tempted to talk about Bustle's pelt unless it was with Frances. She wondered what Frances would do with it. Frances was younger than Dawn's mother and she could tell things about the ship folk that her mother avoided knowing firsthand. Frances would understand that Bustle's pelt was like an old-timer's white beard.

Dawn's mother was waiting inside the Snow Clothing store, conversing with Frances about their favorite subject - that the newcomers, heading north, didn't know how to dress warmly enough for an Alaskan winter. They thought they could endure anything. But they needed the scarves Glenda knitted for selling and the woolen leggings Frances was working on and the fur mittens that Dawn's mother was sewing.

SEVEN

Dawn lived in a house made of lumber so new that it smelled of pine inside. Behind the plank sidewalks where the harbor people hustled along, the road was paved with mud, slush, or snow, depending on the season. Spruce, birch, and blue lupines surrounded the house set under a slope. At the back, the trees were cleared for a raspberry patch, a vegetable garden, and a squat barn that sheltered horses, a cow, and chickens.

After that, the view stretched up to bluish inclines, hare's-tail grass that made waves in the wind under tall masts of spruce. From her bedroom, Dawn could see the ranges of the mountain where streams flowed down near her grandfather's cabin.

"Do you want to sit out back on the porch?" Dawn's mother asked Glenda.

Dawn was already down from the wagon seat, getting the basket of salmonberries that her grandmother brought. Her mother, she knew, spent an awful lot of time on the back porch for a person who had become a townswoman. There were days when she lived more like Grandma Glenda than the folks around her.

"Oh, I don't know, Petra," Glenda said. "I think I felt a raindrop."

At the door, their pushy malamute Reindog met them before Dawn's mother persuaded him to sit down. Then Dawn took him through to the back door and outside where he could spend the afternoon with Uncle Alex's husky, Naomis.

Petra mentioned again, "One of these days, I'll start fixing up a parlor in the room off the hallway."

"Uncle Alex stayed there last night," Dawn said to Glenda. The room wasn't fit for sitting in yet.

"He's been guiding some ship men. They must have had a good day hunting yesterday," Petra added.

"I can't see Alex sleeping in a parlor," Glenda commented.

"He's got other places, the shack where he hunts," Petra said.

"He slept in a boat one night," Dawn put in. "There are so many people in town that Toddy's is probably full."

"Do you think it's stuffy near the stove?" Petra lit up the wood under the coffeepot as Glenda took off her shawl. "I've got a catalog. No, I won't throw any more of it into the stove. Take it with you, Glenda." The large lump of pages plopped onto the kitchen table.

Dawn took her swan plume to the hearth area, divided from the kitchen by only a few beams. Allowing Glenda to tell her mother about the old swan if she chose to, she got out an inkpot from the drawer of the hearth room table. She wasn't quite done with the catalog and its drawing lessons, the raccoon coats and dropped-waist dresses, the phonograph that looked like a huge squash bloom. Because her mother sometimes stuffed the stove with its pages, she had torn out a few pages too.

She perused the catalog's strange wares when her mother was on the back porch. Or when her mother sat near the open window of the room that might become a parlor, watching the town grow as she stitched skin boots and mukluks. When the weather became more brisk and because she didn't think the town was watching her, Petra often wore skin pants. Dawn had found trousers for women in the catalog but they were baggy and made of light cloth.

Since Glenda wasn't requiring her at the kitchen table, Dawn settled into their caribou-hair chair and tested her swan plume.

Petra was saying, "We were talking about a polar bear rug for our parlor."

"There's nothing wrong with having two in your house," Grandma Glenda said.

The catalog pages flipped at the kitchen table. Dawn decided not to venture another opinion since her parents spent an evening arguing over the possible parlor. Around Uncle Alex's cot were heaps of gear, a trap, a gun, and dog harnesses. But now, knotty pine shelves and a varnished rocking chair were on the other side of the room. Slowly the shelves were collecting things that didn't have much use. Wood carvings, a taxidermied squirrel, an old copper pan that Uncle Alex had from the gold days. And on the wall was a length of hide sewn with the Aleut feather pattern, a practice piece that Petra did when she was younger.

There were larger decorations in the hearth room. Of course a salmon was on a plaque, caught on a special day, under which Dawn was bent over the tablet paper, trying a few letters with the quill. Her father had done his letters at home when the weather was bad. Her mother had too because she only went to school when one was close by. When she was Dawn's age, she lived in a cabin somewhere or other because the grandfather Dawn never knew, Grandfather Tuskoffey, made his living by hunting or mining rather than fishing. Soon, the letters under the swan feather looked like decipherable words instead of like those streaked on old Russian signs.

Nobody wrote with quills anymore unless supplies were severely depleted. Uncle Alex said that the one time he took her aboard a ship in the harbor. There she saw a lifelike painting of a moose that the ship captain was taking somewhere. A man named John Audubon had painted it and the captain said that the painter preferred using a swan quill for his drawings. Uncle Alex said then that nobody used swan quills for drawing anymore and that John Audubon had been dead for seventy-five years. Then he said he would get Dawn paints if he happened on them. He was always promising people things and then he forgot the old promise, making a promise to someone new he had met. He didn't know how to make paints the Aleut way and neither did her mother. Uncle Alex knew how to get them from ship people. Usually, Dawn started a drawing with a pencil, reinforcing it with pen or charcoal. If the new quill from Bustle was anything like the old one, she understood why John Audubon drew with a swan quill.

Glenda was saying to Petra, "I don't know why I got a parlor chair if you won't visit us at the inlet. The flowers are blue with forget-me-nots, the moss is thick. Makes me forget that there was ever snow. It's just a cloud on the mountain."

There was a scrape of the coffee pot on the stove. Then Petra replied politely, "I promised Frances mukluks and mittens in the coming weeks. Newcomers are coming on the ships, some going up to Nome. There's so much to observe, what with the new buildings appearing in town. A person has to get used to being a townswoman."

Sometimes Dawn assisted Glenda in her cause, especially since she liked visiting the resident swans in the summer. Or she might suggest that she ride back with Glenda on Lead Boy, her mother's horse. Today though, she had to think how Bustle was no longer at the inlet. She pulled out a pencil drawing from the table drawer, her sketch of Alaska. The map outline resembled a bearded old man with mountain ranges as weathered face lines.

Since she hadn't reminded her mother that she could sew out at the inlet, the kitchen conversation turned to another subject. Glenda broached it with the calm of a swan floating on a lake.

"Did I tell you, Petra, I heard shots on the north side of the lake last spring? During the swan migration. I can't think how people find the inlet, what with the confusion of trails."

"I couldn't tell you," Petra replied as calmly.

"I can't say if swans are being poached. Yet there come less every year."

~~~

Glenda's speech could lap on and on like water at the shore. When she came to their house, she often repeated whatever she had told Dawn on the wagon there. Having so much time alone at the inlet, she looked forward to her coffee with Petra.

She was saying she thought a bear cub crossed the wagon road but it was only a wolverine although they weren't much welcome near the shore where Bustle had come back like a guardian angel these last many years. And it was hard to tell, but the old swan died, not from a wolverine but from old age, collapsing after the rain. Somehow, her mate, Sir Swan, hadn't migrated back at all. But Pinion and Minion were well with four cygnets and there was a swansong before Bustle was gone. Today though, thinking how a wolverine never got the best of Bustle, Glenda almost shot it but then it might have been a bear cub after all and she might have enraged its mother. No, it was best to let Wallop decide even if he lurched so that she would have shot into the air anyway.

Then Glenda said that she'd had enough coffee and she should think about being on her way.

"This plume is the perfect length," Dawn announced, having stilled a shudder at Glenda's mention of a mother grizzly. She took her picture over to the table.

"Old man Alaska," Glenda said, admiring the writing under the map outline.

"Icicles on the beard," Petra said and then she pointed. "And there we are."

"That's his Adam's apple," Dawn said.

"I hope you haven't forgotten the cable stitch I taught you, Dawn," Glenda said.

"Frances knows it."

They all went outside and while Petra woke up Wallop with some garden cabbage, Glenda put her finger on her lips. Then Dawn and her mother gave the wagon two heaves to get it out from the road rut.

Although Wallop took his roundabout route on the way home, Glenda reached her cottage without seeing the shadow of a bear. She showered sunflower seeds and corn on the shore for Pinion and Minion and their cygnets, half-hidden in some overhanging bracken across the bay. They hadn't been coming for the feed since Bustle died. Finally, she went inside to pore over the catalog Petra had given her.

"You'll never guess who will come to possess the swan pelt," Glenda said to Fen when he came in from fishing.

"Someone I know?" Fen said, wary. "Didn't Alex Tuskoffey buy it?"

"No. Your son bought it. He's giving it to Petra. He even talked of having a hat made out of it."

"Petra!" Grandpa Fen grinned. "Do you think Petra is a woman who wants a fancy hat?"

"She wears a nice fur hat. And Petra lives in a town."

EIGHT

It was almost as if Bustle's pelt was forgotten in the next weeks because Young Fen didn't speak of it, not even if Dawn inquired. He only inquired back, asking if Petra spent time at Frances's store that day. If Dawn could invent a reason to spend time with Frances alone, Frances would tell her about it. Dawn also had another secret that she wanted to discuss with Frances rather than her mother.

Uncle Alex had stayed a few days longer after the swan pelt was sold because a ship had arrived. One morning, after eating flapjacks, he said that he was going over to the harbor and then to the General Store before he went on a hunting trip as guide. He had been telling about a shipment to the General Store and a new catalog that Reynolds ordered, selling all sorts of furnishings and school supplies. Dawn might order paints from it, he speculated. In the afternoon, Dawn persuaded her mother that she could get a supply of strong thread at the General Store along with the raisins her father liked on his flapjacks.

She took the road that led up near the smokehouse back door as she often did and then walked behind the buildings to the store. When she asked Mr. Reynolds about the catalog, he said that crates were still being unloaded at the ship. Too often, there were things on the ships that didn't come into the store as told and that was because the ship was on its way to a larger port, usually Sitka or Juneau. Mr. Reynolds hadn't seen Alex yet but his hunting party had been purchasing crackers and beef jerky.

Dawn went out to the verandah and thought she saw Uncle Alex. Although she wasn't supposed to go down to the harbor without him, she hurried towards the muddy shoreline until she saw sailors unloading the ship and that one had a dark jacket like Uncle Alex's sealskin.

She turned back but a sailor accompanied her, asking about accommodations and saying how he'd like to sleep in a bed for a night.

"Someone else knows better," she replied the way her mother did on the boardwalk.

She hurried ahead of the sailor to the store and then, while she was purchasing the thread and raisins, saw that he'd followed her in and was watching her. He wasn't very old but he had wide shoulders. When she was behind the buildings, halfway to the smokehouse, he caught up with her and pulled a braid. This sailor wouldn't let go though and when he twirled her around, he got hold of the other braid. At the end of her braids, he felt to see if she had a bosom.

"My father is twenty paces away," she said.

Talking of paces often went with gun accuracy, she knew from listening to Uncle Alex. And it could scare a sailor since most weren't allowed a gun on board ship.

At the smokehouse, she looked for the man from the back door window. He had disappeared while she decided it would be pointless to tell her father about him. That would lead to hours of sewing at home.

The week that her mother could start harvesting her carrots and beets, Dawn frustrated herself with the cable stitch that Glenda used for winter sweaters. Her mother had another pair of fur mitts for the Snow Clothing store where Frances was spending a quiet day.

There weren't any ships in the harbor, only the boats of the town fishermen, and Frances was doing her work in the back. Frances's father was out setting traps for the game that was feasting on the late summer berries.

Frances studied Dawn's cable stitch and then Dawn asked her if she was making anything out of Bustle's swan pelt.

"I told your mother that my father came by it. That he bought it from an old friend who said the swan died of old age. Well, Petra knew I was speaking of Glenda. Then I said he lost it in a card game to one of those mining men. But the mining man didn't want to be caught selling it. So he asked me to make something for his girl in Seattle. A whole swan pelt for one girl!"

Frances's smile kept itself from laughter but that often caused another to laugh. The idea of a swan pelt being made into an article of clothing was as strange as borrowing the Northern Lights. In catalogs, the print promised that a dress would shimmer or stun people with dyes of every color and sewn-in pearls that weren't really pearls.

Frances continued, "I was afraid your mother would think that the pelt could be made into a fancy cape. But she doesn't think that way. She couldn't understand why the girl in Seattle wouldn't want to do something herself with the feathers."

"Swan feathers are mostly used for hats," Dawn said. Only native men would make a swan pelt into a cape and that would be for ceremony.

"We came to the idea of a hat, all swan. Your father wanted a memento instead of plucking the whole thing. Come here, Dawn. Here are the pieces we're working on."

In a locked drawer was a large piece from Bustle's chest, some of its long feathers plucked so that the down and shorter feathers would cover the head. There were three other strips of hide with feathers, cut for attaching to the main piece. Dawn didn't look long at Bustle's hide being cut like a snowshoe hare's. When Frances saw that, she pulled the drawer out farther so that Dawn could see the rest of the pelt and the long soft feathers.

Unraveling the cable stitch, Dawn thought about Grandma Glenda wanting her to learn Irish knitting. Her mother, being older than Frances, wore skirts from patterns that she obtained from Glenda. Frances liked the newer patterns because she said the men teased her and if she wore something becoming like the women back east, it gave them a sense of propriety.

She wore a flannel skirt that was sleek with her blouse, both of them formed with darts that made her look smart and adamant. Dawn's mother still wore gathered blouses. Frances's hair, wound up, had soft brown lights at the top, and her soundless smile made people laugh. It didn't matter what she did, the men would probably tease her anyway even though she'd been disappointed by one. He had gone on a ship down to California, hearing of the mining there, and hadn't yet returned. Dawn's mother warned her not to ask about him. Frances had waited long enough, so long that she had little confidence in the men who came through town. She still said she was waiting for someone. Now it seemed that she waited for Uncle Alex because he trapped with her father. And Uncle Alex wasn't noticed for teasing women.

There were men who did worse than teasing, Frances knew.

Dawn asked her, "Do you think people would tease someone wearing a hat of swan around here?"

"If you want to know a secret, I think the hat is going to be a memento. Like a wedding dress. Down in Seattle, they have fancy parties that people like the Helsunk's attend. We're trying to make it after a fashion, not the kind of hat to attract teasing."

Probably, it was Frances who knew the difference.

"There are women who have come into money fashionably up in Anchorage and a few here too," Frances continued. "Well, I might wear a hat like that for occasions. There's nothing wrong with special attire, only if a woman wears it for strangers. Now your mother, she feels bad about the old swan being made after a fashion. She's very fussy about it."

Dawn knew her mother would revere a dead swan and that she favored their feathers for her native shirt pattern. But she had said that the spirit of the swan was like a cloud near a mountain peak, like the passing of things on the strong land. Swans seemed to make her mother sad.

Dawn recalled her father's worry. "To most people, swans are no different from mink or the snowshoe hare you wear. Except for the law about them."

"There's the difference. Glenda can be trusted on that. I wouldn't work on that pelt if just anyone brought it in. I don't need that kind of money."

"A man offered me money," Dawn said abruptly. "I wonder if I should ride a horse into town when a ship is in port. But I don't want to tell about it."

Frances stopped knitting at the sweater she was working on. "I'll keep it to myself. Tell me about it."

Frances had been heard more than once to say that she didn't need the money to be with a man she didn't want.

Dawn told her about the braid-pulls of the sailor behind the General Store.

"Did you show him to your father?"

"I didn't see him again."

"You didn't like the look of him, did you?"

"No, I didn't like him."

Sometimes Frances's smile was funny in a shameless way. "Dawn, you ought to be careful. If a man offers you money and you like the look of him, he could become as ugly as any other. You're seeming a young woman to the men who've been traveling. Your braids glow a red that's like maple syrup to those sailors. Some of those women put henna in their hair to get those colors. First they'll ask you over to Toddy's. Or out to their boat or ship."

If there was anything Dawn liked on a fine day, it was sailing in a boat. She had said before that she would like going somewhere on a ship. But there was no resounding reply to that. Even when the ships that came to port were probably sent through Captain Helsunk's shipping interests. He and Mrs. Helsunk were the most fashionable people in town because they had seen places so grand that Alaska was just a salmon to the whales of the other ports.

"Well, at least the men can't walk around so drunk anymore. The deputy means to stop a lot of things with Prohibition. You'll have to wear a hat more often, the right sort of one," Frances said, her knitting needles whirring. She didn't relish a few of the women who came into her store from Toddy's. She said they were women who preferred money over the men who left them there. It had all started, she said, when a man took away Toddy's woman with money, and then, Toddy found himself another woman. Then the man with the money left Toddy's old woman at his establishment. She allowed other abandoned women to stay who were supposed to be a comfort to each other. But then, they were supposed to comfort lonely sailors.

Dawn's mother said the women had nowhere to go because they were always being left. Years ago, when the United States bought Alaska, Russians left their children and the Aleut women who lived with them like wives. But they went on like widows and took to fishing. "And don't think those girls over at Toddy's don't have' ta work hard, Dawn," her mother said. "They cook and clean up after those men. You've seen them with their laundry and chopping wood. Inside, they're sewing their worn-out garments. They don't have one good man to please."

Frances continued, "Still, anywhere you go, on a horse or not, you should be where a man like your father is handy. A bad man has nowhere to go here if he incenses the other men."

Dawn had heard of men thrown out of Toddy's and how they were told they'd better get back on a boat rather than travel north without a friend. If they tried to get Uncle Alex for a guide, he said he didn't go farther than the daylight with someone he didn't trust.

Frances murmured over her knitting, "It's best not to part from those men you know unless they're giving a blessing to the man you've come to know."

"Uncle Alex too?"

Frances's front teeth showed more than a smile which made Dawn giggle.

"Why he's a touchstone, Dawn. He tries the men who love gold to see if they should have it. I often take his advice."

Dawn began her cable stitch again, wondering what her father would say to that.

NINE

Frances had to wonder what Alex would think about the finished cloche-fashion hat. Dawn looked so doubtful, seeing the pieces stretched on a board.

In Alaska, the ornamentation on native parkas was as showy as feathers. If Petra were to wear a hat with swan on it, a unique construction would be best. That was what Frances could do with fur. Of course, Young Fen hadn't meant the hat to unfurl in a beckoning way and with bold ribbons, what a woman might wear in the evening at Toddy's. Frances didn't make anything good enough for them if they had the money for a catalog hat.

When it came to fur, she could form a hat to most tastes since it was the fur that mattered. Her idea for the swan hat was like that.

Young Fen had a feeling of possession about the pelt since he grew up with the swan. Still, he wouldn't ask for a memento made from his dog's fur. She was afraid that, however she made the hat, the memento might make little sense to either Petra or Alex.

This time last year, Frances had gone out to the traps with her father and Alex. They'd gone to the bottleneck that led to the bay where Fen and Glenda lived. When her father was checking one of his traps, Alex pointed at a swan floating on the water. He crept along the shore and said, "Let's follow it," in his rustling woods whisper.

"It's one of the resident swans. Not a swan to shoot."

"You know I'm not thinking of that, Frances."

"You've shot swan up north though, haven't you?"

The swan floated obliviously as Alex paused behind a tree overhanging the shore. "That I have. Let's see if it swims away. It's not often that I don't find caribou or polar bears up north."

"I've never seen you selling swan," she admitted.

"The trading's not what it was in Nome now that Russia is refusing it. The communists are. That's why I come back here."

"I s'pose it's small pickings down here."

"I'd rather hunt than trap. Brought you a reindeer from Kodiak Island along with the bear I sold. Plenty of deer up near Sitka."

Alex Tuskoffey was always looking for better hunting grounds. That was one reason why he guided men as far as Fairbanks and in the fall, went up to Nome for the arctic animals.

"See, it's staying in the same place. Swimmin' round it. C'mon, Naomis." Alex seemed to be talking only to his dog. He began walking along the shore, closing the distance between him and the swan.

"Why are you stalking it?" Frances followed behind him, perplexed.

"It's basking. Like they do in the freezing water up north. Making plans with their mates to cover hundreds of miles. They're like polar bears, basking on ice floes, swimming farther than a kayak. Underneath the snow covering, the ground is like rock. The eyes of a swan tell it. Like a native story."

They were reaching the swan now but it floated farther away from the shore.

"What native story?"

She saw that Alex was beginning to hold his gun in preparation to shooting.

"White birds became people to a hunter. They gave him shelter and a polar bear fur to cover him in the night. When he woke in the mornin', he was on hard ground. The fur wasn't covering him and the birds were gone."

"He was dreaming in the Northern Lights and the birds flew away."

"He wanted the life of a bird. See, it's what I thought. Look down the shore. There are the cygnets."

"You think it would sacrifice itself?"

"No, I think the swan's marking game. A wolverine or a fox. One of these swans led me to a grizzly."

Frances was incredulous. For all Alex's show of superstition, he found game. Now he motioned for her to stay where she was standing and for his dog to go forward. They crept into the bracken and then Frances could see Naomis launching herself. Alex ran into the woods and then she heard gunshot.

The swan flew up into the air. Feeling sympathy, Frances began walking back along the shore, looking for her father. She thought of Paul and his last letter, back in the spring. It sounded as though he was well enough, finding employment at a mining company in California. All he wrote about was the mine and how he'd promised them a year, being useful with his carpentry skills. He'd become friends with the owner's son and they hoped to build a small town around the mine. But he hadn't written to her about traveling to California. It wasn't like the swans. There was only an old promise that he'd come back to her.

She heard a rustle in the leaves. Alex, empty-handed.

"Missed the fox," he said.

"Oh, you're just fooling. To say the swan led you to one."

"Well, the trap got me a snowshoe hare. Up in Nome, some few White Russians have come over, haunted like that swan. Like those promises made too many miles over water. They used to be rich before the revolution in Russia. Now all the aristocrats might have is a piece of jewelry."

He peered at her, his mustache hiding his suspicions. Like most people, they refrained from telling much about their pasts. But Alex gave Frances a sensation of zest. He was as foreboding as the land, blending into the boats and the mountainside like any other man and then in company, puzzling a person with the flickerings of a wonderful hope. He had spent many a night watching the twilight rainbow in the sky. Her father made sure she didn't spend an evening alone with him.

"Is there still gold up in Nome?"

"There's gold! Fur and miles of sledding. I wonder where there's more gold, here or California?"

Frances couldn't say and then they heard the crack of a gun. They walked back to the horses and soon enough, her father was standing before them, ceremoniously displaying a fox he had shot. "Got a mink from one of the traps, too. Saw the fox tail first, like a pheasant."

"I flushed it out," Alex said.

"You'd like pheasant hunting, Alex. Well, my wife is talking me into going back to Manitoba."

"Sounds like sittin' down to a meal. Not like hunting ptarmigan," Alex said.

~~~

Frances told Dawn a little of this while she knitted her cable.

"That must have been Bustle or Sir Swan," Dawn said. "They nested on that side of the bay. They had only two cygnets last year. But it might have been one of the other pair. I suppose they can sense when an animal's in the woods, following their cygnets."

They were sitting behind the counter when Petra came in.

"It's taken you some time to learn a cable stitch, Dawn."

"And it's a quiet day," Frances greeted her. "Dawn can put a cable down a muffler."

"I'm going to need more fur for boots," Petra said.

"I'm about ready to tack the swan feathers down so they won't fall out of that hat, Petra. The pieces have been stretching on the board. With your extra set of hands."

They went to the back room where Frances unlocked the drawer with the pelt in it. Both Frances and Petra leaned over the back table so that Dawn could hardly see the gleaming swan feathers.

Frances said, "My mother is appalled. 'All those feathers at the brim, Frances!' I said, 'They might wear pheasant like that back in Manitoba.' 'That looks like it should be for a wedding,' she said. At least it got her off the subject of Manitoba. She's nearly talked my father into going back there."

Finally Frances stood aside so that Dawn could admire the hat's assemblage. But instead of talking about it, she told about Manitoba. Her parents both came from the fur trade with the Hudson Bay Company but now there were farmers on the plains. A man couldn't farm without having a wife. There were so many women there that they feared they wouldn't be chosen by one of the farmers. That's what her mother missed, her relatives and all the talk about who was marrying, who was expecting, and what old maid would be helping at the next gathering. "She's been trying to refresh me on a whole rigging of conduct that women don't follow here."

Frances didn't want to go back to Manitoba. She said that if Paul didn't return, he was just a river that didn't give over any gold. Now she was capable of sensing whether a man was fooling or if he was the thing that wouldn't tarnish. Some kept their word and paid up as agreed for the tanned hide.

"And they're afraid of me being tempted over to Toddy's," she said. "It's a sore subject at supper."

They heard the door at the front. Frances went out to the counter.

"Miss Banrath! How are you doing this summer?"

With the pieces of Bustle in front of her, Dawn didn't want to talk to her teacher at school. Her mother's dark eye wasn't commanding it; she was looking at fur pieces. They both knew that Miss Banrath gardened at her house behind the school in the summer.

"I've been working on a new skirt and jacket for school this fall," they could hear her.

"Oh, that's a nice tweed," Frances said.

"Yes. I sent for it. When it comes to buttons and lapels, I thought some brushed leather would be nice. Here's the tweed."

"That's easy," Frances said. "I've got some leftover pieces, usually for hat ties and buttons."

Frances came into the back room and pulled out another drawer with deerskin in it. "One of your students, Dawn O'Raine is here. She's learning cable stitch," she said, going back to the counter.

Dawn went out and said, "Hello, Miss Banrath."

"That's a fine way to spend a day like this, Dawn. It's beginning to drizzle. Are you doing any reading this summer?"

Dawn paused. She hadn't read much except for the catalog. "I've been practicing letters. And drawing."

"You're in good health, Miss Banrath?" Frances asked.

While Miss Banrath became as intent over the deerskin and the tweed as if they were spelling papers, Dawn disappeared to the back room. Miss Banrath was on the watch for bad health, her students knew. Mrs. Helsunk said she had smallpox when she was a girl and that accounted for the little scars on her face. Minister Calvert signed her on for school teaching when she lived in a fishing town near Seattle. Frances found out from the minister that her young man there had spent a year in a sanitarium before he declined from tuberculosis.

"Oh yes," Miss Banrath was answering. "If people wear rain clothing, the summers here can be rejuvenating. I suppose you don't see so many people with the ague now."

"No, just sailors with the scurvy. They don't come in so often. I guess you're not thinking about returning to Washington."

"I've promised another year. It's hard for the minister to find a replacement. And I've heard by letter that my brother is speaking of coming up here. He's found out about a place in the Juneau cannery."

"Well, that's a nice thing!"

"He'd rather come up here than work at a Seattle cannery," Miss Banrath said.

"Now didn't you hear of it at the Salmon Annual?"

"I heard they were in need up there of a man for their export office. One that could read and write. All he needs to do is to write a nice letter."

Frances said, "My mother's been talking my father into going back to Manitoba. I tell you, Miss Banrath, I'm too used to being here. I'm afraid they'll have to tie me up and bag me to take me there."

Dawn heard a rare laugh come out of Miss Banrath. Frances's pouting grin must have brought it on. Davy Shamison said funny things to her all the time at school and she never laughed. Her mother caught her eye, comprehending how it was at school. Then she moved the pieces of swan around so that Dawn might see how the hat would look.

TEN

A few weeks later, as summer began to shiver, Petra opened a yarn box that contained her birthday present. Uncle Alex had returned from another hunting journey for the occasion and with a hare for his sister's birthday dinner. Frances was there to watch Petra open the present that she helped to fashion. She admired the native shirt that Petra wore for the occasion, sewn with feathers across the front.

Petra sat in their caribou hide chair after dinner. She made Dawn and the dogs impatient while she wistfully unknotted a fir-green hair ribbon that bound the yarn box. Then Dawn had to hold Reindog and Naomis, keeping them on their haunches while her mother opened the box.

"What!" she said, as if she weren't sure that the right gift had gotten into the right box. Then her dark eyes narrowed from disbelief. But Frances and Young Fen didn't say that she hadn't seen right.

"The swan bonnet!" she finally said. "You were making it for me and not for a miner's girl in Seattle?"

Frances laughed. "You know those roustabouts that come through and convince me to sew something nice for them. Their intentions amount to a fortune."

"You mean he didn't want it after we made it?" Petra held the hat on her balled-up hand. She twirled it slowly for Dawn and her father, like a weathervane on a breezy day.

"No, we were fooling you, Petra," Young Fen said. "Didn't you admire the hat when it took shape? I wanted you to like it."

"For a miner's girl in Seattle, I admired it," Petra replied. Her face was flushed and she looked uncertain, as if she expected the hat to melt like mountain snow.

"I thought Frances would say that it was for a sailor's girl. It's shaped like a southwester hat." Young Fen smiled enough for his mutton chops to retract.

Dawn inspected the hat as her mother thanked her father for it. The hat was brimmed, what Frances called a cloche hat. Its brim was fringed with feathered pieces that made a ducktail in the back while the crown of the hat was thick with swan's down and small feathers. It was as nice-looking as anything Dawn had seen drawn in a catalog.

Abruptly, Petra plopped the swan hat on her head. She might have clapped a cloud around her since her face was flushed as a sunset. The feathers in the shirt and those at the hat brim made a picture.

"But where would I wear this hat?" Petra wondered, taking a stride to a window where she could see her reflection. The feathers ruffled in the air until she held the hat by its thin leather ties. Then she fastened the straps at her neck. "It might not get so soggy as fur in wet weather. But I think it could be a joke in town."

From his seat near the fireplace, Uncle Alex said sullenly, "You should oil the feathers once in a while the way a swan would."

"I don't see that it's much different from a polar bear hat," Young Fen said. "You have a story 'bout that hat like Uncle Alex has a story about his lump of gold. If people joke about it, tell them how lucky you are to have a swanskin since swans can't be shot legally anymore. Tell 'em the swan died of old age. You must like that hat. You helped to fashion it."

"I like the hat fine. It's not something for everyday though." Petra hardly ever said things to be polite.

Then Dawn saw that Reindog and Naomis had their muzzles near the open box that once held skeins of yarn. When she pushed them away, she saw a feather teasing them. In the box was a layer of hide and feathers.

"The rest of the pelt is in here!" Dawn said.

"Now I suppose *you* want a swan hat," her mother said, amused but wary. "We can sew the feathers into a shirt."

Trying her mother's hat on was one thing, Dawn didn't say. Wearing a native shirt with a feather pattern was another thing, not what she would do on a school day. But since the feathers were Bustle's, she wouldn't mind practicing the traditional sewing with them.

"You wouldn't wear a hat like this," her mother accused her.

"I couldn't even touch Bustle before this summer. But couldn't we weave one of her feathers in a hat for me?" Dawn replied.

"You could put feathers in the band of your straw hat," Young Fen answered. "Those feathers are too nice to stuff anything except a parlor pillow. There's not really much use for swan feathers, is there, Alex?"

"People want them," Uncle Alex replied. "But Captain Helsunk said he wanted a sleigh. I told him I could start building one and meantime he bought a motorcar!"

Still amazed, Dawn's mother untied the swan hat and put it in the box. She then put it in a hall cupboard out of Reindog's reach and when she returned, a raspberry cake Frances made was on the hearth table.

"We already have stories to tell about that hat, don't we, Frances?" Petra said.

~~~

Frances recounted, "I've never worked with a material that kept flexing as if it meant to flap away. The hide recoiled from my needle and the top feathers bristled. I didn't like plucking them out but I plucked so that the feathers would lie along the brim right. And I sewed some in. I suppose Petra's right about attending to such a hide in a natural way."

The hearth fire glinted off their knives and forks as Frances spoke.

"That's why I stitched some straps on even if the cloche hats usually don't have them. I had reason to fear that the swan hat might sail off of Petra's head."

Uncle Alex scuffed his boots on the firestones, interrupting Frances.

Writing with a swan plume took practice, Dawn knew. She wanted Frances to go on since she never sewed anything that wasn't for learning mukluks or skirts. "Was it hard to attach the feather pieces on the brim?"

"Well, I had to cut another piece before I was through. So that the feathers swayed back the way they do. I'm proud to tell you that I've never worked with swan much."

Young Fen put in, "Don't you think it'll be dry as a southwester rain hat?"

"Dry as a bone," Frances agreed. "And then when I was saying how the hat was for a miner's girl in Seattle, the feathers tickled my nose. So that set me off laughing and sneezing. I thought Petra would suspect something."

Petra said, "I had my own troubles with it. I was trying to stitch the edges but the feathers flexed in front of my needle so I couldn't see what I was doing any more than if I was in a blizzard."

Uncle Alex sighed and wheezed so wearily that Dawn hoped he was snoring. But then he took a slurp of his coffee, his black mustache showing its usual scornful expression. He wasn't disdainful when Dawn listened to his stories about hunting and trapping in the north. Still he had the look of a snare in the night snow, saying, "You were spooked at swan feathers, Frances! How does a swanskin differ from any other hide once the wearer is gone? I would have thought you'd tell such a story 'bout a grizzly hide while a storm was roaring outside. If you're gonna have such respect for an animal's hide, then let its spirit go." He loosened his boots and warmed his red-stockinged feet at the fire.

Frances reached for her handbag of Snow Clothing knitting.

"A swan has a stubborn spirit. Even a hard spirit," Uncle Alex said, and began one of his arduous accounts. "You don't know what being spooked is, Frances. A person gets dazed with crystal and the lights that are just the spirits of summer. Up north if it weren't for the dogs, I sometimes think I'm on the ghost of the world. If I didn't use what died, I'd slip to the other side. Just to find the ghost of the brown bear."

"All you havta do is wave a piece of white flannel in front of Alex and he'll up and grab his gun," Young Fen laughed. "And he says he's seen White Russians up there in Nome. All the trouble with trading and the Red Russians right now."

"How can you tell a White Russian?" Dawn wondered. "Don't they sneak in?" She had heard of the rich Russians who lost their money in the Russian Revolution. They were aristocrats, not folks like her grandfather Tuskoffey.

"Anyone who can speak Russian in Nome these days might be fleeing Russia," Uncle Alex said. "They don't want to stay in Nome though. The Reds, the communists, won't do business with us anymore. In my father's time, there was a regular trade with Russia.. That's why I'm bringin' the furs back around to Anchorage. I don't know if I'll make the journey this fall," Uncle Alex said, scratching at the saber tip of his moustache. "It's hard to find the right partners. I don't sleep through things like my sister does. And you know what swindlers men can be down here, Frances. I won't go on a bobsled journey unless I've shown the gold nugget from my hidden pocket and given the other man a chance to swipe it. If they don't, I'll travel with them. But not a few have disrupted my sleep. Still, men are better than animals in snow clothing. The bear bares its teeth for the seal and the seal for the fish."

"Swans don't eat other animals," Dawn commented.

"That's why they can't stay the winter," Uncle Alex replied.

"At least animals won't swipe your gold nugget, Alex," Frances said.

Uncle Alex sneered. Then he peered at Frances and asked, "Something fiercer than a human would. Did I ever tell you how my parents died?"

ELEVEN

Frances hauled a length of hearth-orange knitting from her bag and murmured, "I guess I haven't heard much about that. And an old-timer too."

Dawn's mother began collecting cake plates. The silverware chattered like teeth, interrupting Uncle Alex from recounting the tragedy. She called for Reindog and around her, cupboard doors whapped shut, the dogs scrabbled for scraps, the dishes made a din.

"Seems that you could tell Frances 'bout that over at Toddy's sometime," Young Fen said.

"Seems that I'm leaving for some time early tomorrow," Uncle Alex replied.

Dawn fidgeted with her bootlaces. She wanted to hear her uncle's version of the disaster that her parents summed up with the word *avalanche.* Now her mother was doing her own birthday dishes. Tugging up her socks, Dawn wondered why the dish washing had to be so ill-timed.

Tonight though, her father said, "It's getting late, Dawn. I'll help your mother with those dishes. That'll be a birthday present for sure. Too bad your uncle seems to have forgotten whose day it is."

"Petra's birthday is about her mother too," Uncle Alex grumbled.

That put Dawn in mind of Bustle and the birthday bonnet. She was as drawn to Uncle Alex's low voice as if she had seen smoke across waters. He started his telling with dire descriptions of glacier-glazed mountain peaks. "I thought that spring snows were like sand and always blew away then. But they can come solid so a person has to pick at them as if they're limestone. But I wasn't fifteen-years-old and Petra wasn't sixteen yet. We went first thing that spring to a mining cabin. With the swans, as my mother used to say. There was copper north of Anchorage and possibly gold. Bears had broken the ice on the river nearby."

Uncle Alex's voice became strained like wind at the window as he went on. "Our cabin was downhill from where my father, Dmitri Tuskoffey, found that he had to use dynamite. I thought the precipices above us were all rock. They were titanic snow-covered hailstones, I learned. Ice. And the mountain snow is the kind that splinters the way mirrors break."

Dawn kicked off her boots and sat on the bearskin rug where Reindog was hoarding a bone. Next to her Frances rocked, mesmerized over ripples of orange wool.

"Did you go to the mountain mines every year?" Frances asked.

"Since I was old enough to help my father, we did," Uncle Alex said. He looked askance at Frances as if he were thinking that she heard many such tales at the counter of Snow Clothing. "My father maintained us on whatever was plentiful. And most of what he did, alone as he was among men, was with a collection of learning and know-how. He was brought up on a Russian Orthodox mission after his father died. He probably didn't confer enough about dynamite and it was pretty new then."

Uncle Alex pulled at the frown on his moustache before going on. "We had just opened up a vein in the mountain when a freak spring storm began. In our cave, we couldn't see how bad it was getting. By the time we got down to the cabin, the snow had gobbed a muffler around it. We shut ourselves up inside. We'd discovered copper and calculated getting to it within a month.

"By the second day, we couldn't have left unless we abandoned our horse and wagon. We had a sled and a few dogs too. But it was a heavy, insulatin' snow. It swirled the ground into a surface like shale and that dense."

Frances got up from her chair. "In Manitoba when I was a girl, a winter didn't go by without the snow stranding us inside for some days. A drift of wool turned into a pile of sweaters. We were never stranded under a mountain though. Would you hold out your arm a minute, Alex?"

Uncle Alex stretched out his arm while Frances measured her knitting on it but soon enough, he shrugged off the draping yarn.

"No mountains and you didn't use sleds," Alex said.

"We depended on snowshoes. And a sledge." Frances held down Alex's wrist.

"Horses in deep snow. You don't have to be so exact since the sweater's not for me," he complained. Then he heaved himself onto the firestones as if his memory chilled him.

"You're the yardstick to tell by around here," Frances demurred.

"My mother was brought up Aleut Indian. Her father returned to Russia after the United States bought the territory. She wasn't one to hibernate whether it was sea squalls or snow. That night while I slept in that snow, I dreamt of the dynamite. But when I awoke, I found that the explosions of rock and snow were real. They broke the walls of the cabin! My far corner, where we kept the dogs, was blasted with wind. I shouldered my way through the gusts, the dogs leapin' at me too, and found Petra in a slumber of snow. But her sleeping bag was against a wall that still stood. Then I saw that one of the cabin walls *was* snow and Petra had been knocked out cold by an avalanche!"

From her spine, Dawn heard the dishes clattering in the kitchen.

Gruffly, he went on, "I dragged Petra out from the impact. She came to after I shook her. I was struck dumb looking at the block of snow that came in like a treacherous tide. The roof was caving in and a gale with stinging ice made it hard to see. Petra and I kept looking for our parents' fur sleeping bag but a jagged slant of lumber, caked with a mortar of snow, was in the way. That's all that was on that side of the cabin - a burial mound.

"There was nothin' to do but use a pick and a shovel. I kept thinking how our dynamite probably loosened the boulders above us. Petra was in a frenzy and I wondered if she was all there. She threw herself at the wreckage of timber and ice, tearing at it with her bare hands. Might as well try to smash a lock. The dogs jumped and yelped with us."

Petra appeared with some strong-smelling spruce logs. She tossed them on the fire and they blazed Uncle Alex off of the firestones. Then she made some conversation with Alex about the parlor room and flannel sheets.

But Uncle Alex didn't take the hint. He finished his tragic telling.

"We buried them at the nearest settlement. It weren't one where we ever lived. I didn't go back for the copper after the storm. Death was a cold tyrant, cunning enough to wear white and cold enough to turn tears into jewels. Petra had bouts of sleepwalking after that. Nightmares, I guess. Maybe she'd be more clear about it if she didn't stop me from tellin' what's true."

Dawn watched the spruce log. If she went upstairs now, she would shiver in her sheets, thinking about her mother becoming an orphan. She puzzled about her grandparents. There were no photographs of them.

"Then you worked on a salmon boat, didn't you, Uncle Alex?" Dawn asked, hoping he would start talking again. Frances was still shaking her head and making remarks that clicked with her knitting needles. She often shared woes at Snow Clothing.

Coming out of the kitchen, Young Fen said, "The same one I worked on."

"You tell Frances about working on the salmon boat, Petra," Uncle Alex said.

This actually stopped Frances's knitting and she waited for Petra with expectant eyes. She wouldn't be getting up to end the evening around the hearth.

TWELVE

Petra came in from the hallway with Naomis. She didn't seem to mind taking up the next part of the fireside story.

"We had to earn our bread. There was little to recover besides that gold nugget. Alex didn't want to work in a fish cannery. I couldn't hunt with him, there were so many ruffians, even the man that our father knew. But I was at my full height and in a grizzly hat, I could pass for a boy. Our mother came from fishing people and I knew as much as Alex. So I got hired as Alex's brother on a salmon boat. I mended nets."

Frances picked up her knitting again, looking bemused about her eyebrows. Dawn could see that for once, she was really astonished at someone's account of themselves. Ever since Dawn heard this about her mother, she longed to stand on the deck of a ship, wearing a sunflower-yellow slicker and a southwester hat. She'd been fishing plenty of times in a dinghy and although the work was hard on the hands, she liked the freedom of the talk out on the water and the occasional sight of a whale.

Frances commented, "I'd probably be bothered less if I disguised myself in Snow Clothing. Having a shotgun near the till and my father a call away doesn't sink into some men's heads. What name did you go by on the fishing boat?"

"They called me Peter," Petra said.

"They called her witless enough to walk on water," Uncle Alex snorted. "I told the crew that her head was affected from a concussion. So she was left to herself, mending nets and cleaning fish. She had on such a bulk of fishing clothing that she looked like a lumpy halfwit. One of those painstaking ones."

"Boy, were they the dumb ones," Young Fen said. "They couldn't see that it was the neck of a grown girl in the corner of the boat. I suspected her even if I hadn't known many women besides my mother. They used to call me Swan Boy then 'cause my mother sold swan feathers. I put up with it since I'd gotten to the age where I wanted to get away from my father's cockleshell skiff."

On the bearskin rug, Dawn was pretending to sleep with her head propped on a stool. She used to fall asleep there when Uncle Alex told about his trips late in the evening. The talk usually became so interesting that her parents forgot to argue with her about going to bed and everyone liked to soak in the fire on a cold night. She heard her mother's tread and then a blanket plopped near her. But what her father said next wedged into her mind like an unwelcome occurrence in a dream.

"They called me Swan Boy because I didn't bring a migrating swan to market. Swans were game then but not on our land. Eventually I got so mad that I shot a swan, not a particularly healthy one. My father found out and said I was old enough to work at the harbor and rich enough to feed myself. So I joined the salmon boat."

Dawn gulped some air and covered her mouth with her hand, afraid of making an outcry at what she heard. But her breath came out like the heave of sleep. Only the clicking of needles, almost indistinguishable from the spitting of the fire, answered this.

Her father went on. "I thought that Alex was a wily one. I didn't doubt the tragic avalanche but I didn't believe that Petra was his brother. I could tell when they talked that she was acting barmy on purpose. And she was wearyin' of it. She was awfully deft with her hands for being manacled in all that fishing gear. And her collar up a lot of the time. But she had to lean down when she sorted the catch. Her neck was lithe, like a swan's. I suspected she would never have an Adam's apple or a beard. And her face looked older'n Alex's."

"I teased him about being the swan boy," Alex said.

"The more I talked to Alex, the more leery I got. When we were aground, he and his brother Peter didn't join in with the other fishermen. Oh, they had to go hunting and turn native but Peter, now he could still cook. I'd become pretty sure that he didn't have any barmy brother and that he was covering for someone whose name was not Peter. But I'm a mother's son so I didn't say anything until we were off the boat."

Having heard this part before, Dawn bobbed at the shore of sleep. Waves were joggling her when she became aware again of what was being said. Her uncle was telling about the promise of gold up in Nome and how he had to use an icicle like a knife with a man there. While he told Frances that no amount of snow clothing would give newcomers sense in the tundra, Dawn became aware of the hot bristles of bearskin at her elbows and the fire in front of her. Farther away, Uncle Alex was saying that he had seen hundreds of swans north of Nome. But he might have said seals because Dawn was dreaming of swans in the Northern lights. Her uncle was advising Frances to tell people his worst stories about the wolves and the bear and the icy sea.

THIRTEEN

The swan bonnet stayed in the high storage cupboard where blankets and mufflers were kept. Dawn wanted to see its luster and its feathers so much that she wasn't so sad anymore about the old swan.

"When are you going to wear Bustle's hat?" she asked her mother.

"When there's an occasion." Her mother tugged on her brown hare hat. To wear fashion was to be noticed and her mother didn't need to be noticed by the fishermen that she already knew. She didn't like the wayfarers at the harbor noticing her, their winks mingling with the fishermen familiarity. The fishermen might call her by her first name and get her mixed up with the women at Toddy's who went by their first names with newcomers. Petra had never liked being familiar with the kind of man who might steal Uncle Alex's gold nugget.

Since the strange sailor pulled both of her braids, Dawn considered her appearance on the boardwalk. A shawl knit by her grandmother didn't cause a man to pause the way her waisted hide jacket did. Braids were supposed to mean that she was too young for any of the sailors but some looked as young as the boys in town who went out on the salmon boats in the summer.

Dawn's father pondered an occasion for the swan bonnet. He had only one suit of clothes that didn't smell like the fumes in the salmon smokehouse. Those were the clothes that he wore to church. Sometimes he wore them when a ship was in port and he had smoked salmon ready for export.

"How'd you like to eat at Toddy's today?" Young Fen asked one morning at breakfast. "You're always saying how you like their salmon pastry pies, Petra."

"Isn't Glenda coming into town?"

"She is. And a Mr. Phillips from the ship. He might want to talk over at Toddy's."

"I'll be going, won't I?" Dawn asked.

"If Glenda wants to sit at Toddy's. You'll both want hot chocolate, I guess. You ought to wear your hood with the otter on it, Dawn. It's wet today. Petra can wear the swan bonnet."

"To sit at Toddy's? What would Mr. Phillips think? Halloo?" She imitated one of the town fishermen.

"Mr. Phillips wants to talk about salmon. He's interested in the hunting around here too. I don't mind bringing up the subject of swan and Glenda won't mind telling him what she thinks about it. Toddy's is the only place to eat in the daytime. Besides, I'd like to see you in the hat."

Dawn found a catalog and showed her parents hats that made the swan bonnet look small and easy to wear by comparison. "Look, this one has so many feathers standing up that they'd be dancing."

Her mother said, "It's so. I've seen hats that would make a man feel as if he's got liquor in him if he can't get any. But this one needs explaining and I don't want to explain to Toddy's woman today. Young Fen, I'll wear it to church sometime. It would cover my hair and that would be less of a fuss."

Then the day went by its regular pattern, Glenda coming to the house and Young Fen having his salmon pastry while he conferred with Mr. Phillips.

At home, Petra often left her hair in braids. She complained that her hair was too straight and slippery to put up and that it fell down when she was working. Stray strands escaped the pins so that her head seemed to have stems and leaves in it as she bent over her sewing or her gardening.

Dawn was beginning to think how she would manage her own hair when she stopped wearing braids. Her braids were causing too much teasing and like Frances, she expected that a more sedate style would keep the sailors and the fishermen's sons at school from thinking a braid was flirting with them. A few girls wound their braids on their ears or at the back of their heads but that wasn't the way with Grandma Glenda. Glenda thought hair should be fixed in a neat cap, like the lid of a jar. But that would be to arrange her hair like Miss Banrath. Frances's hair was always in the same wavy rolls because she owned a curling iron. Curling irons could be ordered from the catalog.

The next Sunday, Petra kept her hair in braids though she put on her green twill skirt. If she wore a fur hat, she usually turned her braids up into it. Dawn preferred to wear her straw hat, ornamented with a few swan feathers sewn in, rather than a hood. Her solution about her hair, for the time, was to wear one braid instead of two.

Her father's Sunday hat had an ivory medallion at the front, carved with the crescent of a leaping fish. His hat tipped up as Petra came down the stairs, walking on her boots as softly as if they were moccasins. "Why, it looks like snow on spruce with your twill," he said.

In fact the hat looked small and sleek, setting off Petra's white blouse under her green cloth jacket. Young Fen had already admired the hat upstairs, Dawn could see. She walked around it as her mother tied its leather straps. Then Dawn put on her own straw hat, anticipating their entrance.

There were often folks to note at church, people who attended as infrequently as her grandparents did or people who were staying in town. The church was said to be Episcopal but that didn't matter so much since it was the only church for the fishermen who lived on the coast. Some people were doing well with the canneries, as well as her father was doing with the smoked salmon.

"Remember what we're going to tell people about the hat," Young Fen said as they started out. "I want to know what they ask. It's more than a fashion, Dawn. It's a memento."

Her father's step was measured and light beside her mother's wary tread. His smooth stride made Dawn think of swans gliding and how Bustle used to lead the others, swimming up to the shore. When they reached the boardwalk from the road behind, Dawn could survey anyone who might notice the hat. Her mother was looking ahead and the swan feathers at the brim kept her from admonishing Dawn as they passed Toddy's. Thaddeus's Hotel and Eatery, as it was called since Prohibition, often catered to men who spat tobacco near the door, as they did when it was chiefly a saloon.

Today, Toddy was conversing with a man on the boardwalk and the player piano was going, its plinks like raindrops in the quiet morning.

Often, Toddy would give a yell when he glimpsed them. Their greetings usually went on as they walked. Young Fen was prepared to step out into the harbor road if there was a crowd outside. "Young   Fen and Petra! Come in for a bite after church. The new woman is cooking some fine caribou, came in yesterday!" Toddy would say.

Young Fen usually replied, "It's not the Sunday for my folks," or he'd say, "My folks are coming in and we're fixing on some duck."

"I've got some men looking for a guide," Toddy might call to Petra. "Getting late for church," Petra would answer loudly.

Mrs. Helsunk had asked them to remind Toddy about services. She actually thought Toddy could be converted. Even if he still had a bad odor, he might imbibe some Christian spirit since some of his visitors came to church on Sundays, she often said. Petra didn't mind helping Toddy to put aside his business on a Sunday if he would stop yelling down the boardwalk as if she and Young Fen weren't married. And if there were any women outside, they smiled as if their night social was the thing a person shouldn't miss.

This morning, Toddy stared down the boardwalk until Dawn thought that they might pass by without reminding him about church.

"Mornin' Young Fen!" he finally called. Then he stared at Petra as if he were waiting to be introduced to the person wearing the swan hat.

"Mornin' Toddy!" was all Young Fen replied. Then as they neared the smokehouse, he said, "See, we should have showed him that hat on an afternoon."

~~~

Past Toddy's and the General Store, they strolled in the fresh harbor air where a few people peered at the swan bonnet and even the gulls seemed to mistake it, reeling above.

"I'd say this is an occasion," Young Fen said.

This was so pleasant that they slowed, approaching the door of the white wooden church. The congregation was singing their first hymn as they entered. Reaching a pew was like straddling a trail where overgrowing boughs might poke a person.

If the swan bonnet caused remark, Dawn couldn't tell because the usual murmurs followed the usual snapping shut of hymnals. The potbellied stove in the church sizzled as if it were a warning about hellfire. Other latecomers, stomping in, drowned out any stray talk.

Sitting next to her mother, Dawn would normally be hindered from looking around by a grip on her arm. Church was the only time Dawn ever saw the townspeople in one room. In the old Russian church up in Sitka where her parents were married, icons kept the eyes in one place. Her mother said they made her think about the journeying of people like those in the Bible.

The swan bonnet was allowing Dawn more scope though. Preoccupied with the hat, Petra loosened its ties and tipped her head towards the front of the church. Meanwhile, Dawn swayed while she straightened her coat so that she could see the other churchgoers. People often looked better than they did on the main boardwalk of town because they were cloaked and combed and hatted. Or they looked more scruffy, downcast, and patched because they were wearing their everyday clothes. Dawn didn't glance long though. Most people were looking at the swan bonnet, not at Minister Calvert. Oscar, a boy who was probably on his father's fishing boat all week, stared at the swan bonnet as if it were flying overhead, and Davy Shamison kept looking from it to his father as if he hadn't already seen it.

Petra sat as serenely as a statue, her eyes on the minister. Dawn sat still then too, so still that she heard the sermon while she admired the swerve of the swan feathers beside her. To her, the hat was like Bustle, glistening in the reeds, giving the day a fineness. The minister roused everyone up from their seats, his sermon ending with a warning he made several times a year, the warning about temptation in the wilderness.

As usual, Dawn turned a little as she stood up, looking for Frances this time, but Frances and her parents were surrounded by scruffy-whiskered men in new sweaters. Her mother had to tip her head back to see the hymnal that she shared with Young Fen. Then Dawn saw that the swan bonnet was drifting down from her head. Her mother's braids, which were arranged inside the hat, slid down also. She heard a gasp as the hymn started.

The bonnet slid to her mother's back like the hats of western men but it was still tied on. Behind them, Mrs. Helsunk was glaring so that her eyes looked like the slits in a fancy pie. Townswomen like her only wore braids when they were sleeping.

Dawn nudged her mother and then she pulled her own braid near her face. Her mother stooped in the pew, fixing the bonnet back on her head and tucking her splayed braids inside the collar of her jacket.

At the end of the service, Petra stood stock-still, clutching the pew in front of her. Young Fen stood at attention, his eyes on the minister as if they'd been told to stay after the service. They didn't turn to leave until people had milled out past their pew.

"I think I'll keep this hat for special occasions only," Petra said, venturing down the aisle as if it were a tossing boat. When lingerers admired the hat at the door, she hardly moved her head. "Thank you. I don't know when I'll ever wear it again. I wanted to wear it to church once."

"It's a sight too lovely," Minister Calvert said, extending his hand. "It has swan feathers on the crown too, I see."

Mortified, Petra looked for Frances in the churchyard. Frances was wearing a new hat that had a brim of snowshoe hare fur and two swan feathers as decoration.

"Frances made the hat," Dawn said to the minister. "It's a memento."

"It was made from an old swan," Young Fen explained to him. "She nested all the years I can remember at the inlet. She was sick this summer and died."

"I surely hope that the hat doesn't start any coveting for swanskins," Minister Calvert cautioned.

"That's just it," Young Fen said. "There's been poachin' at the inlet. I might discover who's doing it. The sheriff and the deputy haven't had much time for it. That's why I didn't sell the swanskin to merchants."

FOURTEEN

While her father talked to the minister, Dawn followed her mother to chat with Frances under the awning of a Sitka spruce. They both passed Mrs. Helsunk without realizing that she was calling to them. Mrs. Helsunk hardly ever conversed with Dawn's mother unless it was about Toddy.

"Petra! Petra O'Raine!" Mrs. Helsunk had a commanding tone and her braided cloak had an official look.

The swan hat fluttered slightly as Petra paused, puzzled. Its sheen made her look dressy without all the garnishment that Mrs. Helsunk had. And Dawn thought that her mother's face was pretty to look at because she had high cheekbones like faces in catalog pictures.

"Petra!" Mrs. Helsunk said again, and she overtook them. "I was admiring your hat until the mishap with it. Oh, it's pretty! You're not used to ties, are you? I could show you another way to fasten them." Mrs. Helsunk raised her sleek gloved hands as if she were longing to touch the swan bonnet. But from her plump face, her eyes lowered on the exposed sections of Petra's braids. At least she wasn't staring at her hands as if she should be wearing cloth gloves.

"Frances can show me a way so that the ties don't feel so tight," Petra replied, still perplexed. "She made this hat."

"It's custom-made! That must have made Frances's time at that store more interesting."

Petra replied, "Likely it's one of the last swanskins that you'll see on this continent."

These words must have impressed Mrs. Helsunk, she held herself so stiffly. Then Dawn's mother told her the story about the swanskin and Bustle's sickness. Mrs. Helsunk listened intently but she stared at the hat with a thrilled look.

"Speaking of rules that are supposed to extend to this territory," Mrs. Helsunk said, assured that what she was going to say was more important. "Some of us are starting a temperance society. I want you to come over for coffee so I can tell you about it. My brother, Sheriff Farefax, is going to support the society. Prohibition has been too much for him."

Dawn's gaze swayed to her mother. Uncle Alex often called Sheriff Farefax what others at Toddy's called him - Foamface. He had liked a glass of ale before Prohibition. The burly sheriff, adept with trappers and adventurers and thieves, helped Uncle Alex with anyone who tried to pickpocket his nugget of gold.

The feathers of the swan hat fluttered languidly. Mrs. Helsunk didn't mind speaking to the nodding feathers. She clasped her chained eyeglasses from her heaving chest to peer at them and say a second time, "Won't you come over for coffee and cake? On Saturday. How's one o'clock?" Then she aimed her gold-framed glasses at Dawn. "You can come too."

"Alright. One o'clock on Saturday," Petra said after her pause.

"Prohibition is going so badly here, Petra. What an awful habit alcohol is! Even a girl growing up ought to be informed. With all the ruffians around here. Oh, and you must wear that hat!" Mrs. Helsunk, cumbrous in her rich maroon and citrus-colored braidings, marched over to her husband, Captain Helsunk.

Dawn was eager to see her parlor. "Grandma Glenda's been to Mrs. Helsunk's house. To show her swan plumes."

"She has a real parlor, I heard. Frances has seen it and so has Alex," Petra said.

People hadn't talked much about the inside of the Helsunk's house lately because Captain Helsunk bought a motorcar, sent from Juneau on a ship. Roads were being built near the railroad and he said it wouldn't be long before he could drive to Anchorage. Dawn had seen him driving along the harbor road five times since the spring, usually with someone who had come in on a ship. Anyone who walked too near the car was honked at with a sound louder than a ship's horn and some were afraid that Captain Helsunk wouldn't be able to stop the car.

FIFTEEN

"The hat will be the occasion at Mrs. Helsunk's," Petra said in the hearth room after their Sunday meal. They usually sat like that, Petra and Young Fen at the fire and Dawn at the table where she had the Bible open. Usually Dawn studied the pictures in it and then she compared them with her schoolbooks. Sometimes she read aloud a story that was asked for, usually one about Abraham or Moses or Jesus in the wilderness.

"It's an occasion, visiting her parlor," Dawn said.

"But you can't speak of that. You'll have to let her do the talking," Petra said.

"You'll like wearing the hat in her parlor," Young Fen said, although he hadn't ever sat in it.

Petra wondered, "Did your mother wear her nice hat when she visited Mrs. Helsunk?"

Frances made the hat Glenda wore to church. It had a lace veil and a swan feather sewn in at the brim.

"Now I don't know," he said. "I think she just went over there after she drove the wagon into town."

"What if Mrs. Helsunk wants to buy it?" Petra wondered. "She always wants the best things that come into the General Store."

"It wouldn't look right on her. You tell her it's a memento."

The thought of Mrs. Helsunk in the swan hat made Dawn laugh.

"The pelt meant something to Glenda," Petra said.

"She's got another pair of swans to watch," Young Fen said. "You don't want to wait until the Salmon Annual. And that might not be the occasion."

The summer Salmon Annual was usually the event for dress-up. People from the canneries attended and since they established the price of fish, Young Fen needed to stand up with them to keep his convenient supply. In recent years, he sold smoked salmon to the canneries.

"Having that swan pelt reminds me of the native story that Alex tells," Petra said. "You remember about the hunter, don't you Dawn?"

Dawn remembered. "Uncle Alex acted like a caribou when he told it. That was the part he liked."

"How did that go?" Young Fen stretched his feet towards the hearth.

Petra began, "The hunter left his family because his mother-in-law hated him. When he chanced upon some white birds, he wanted to be one of them. He thought their lives were better."

"They turned into people," Dawn continued. "They gave him a polar bear fur to cover him in the night. When he woke, all he had was two feathers."

"Now I remember," Young Fen said. "He had to learn that the swans had a hard life."

Dawn continued, "Then he wanted to be a snowshoe hare but the same thing happened. But when he wanted to be a caribou, the caribou let him be one of them."

Recalling how Uncle Alex cavorted as if he had the antlers of a caribou made them all forget the mishap with the swan bonnet. But finally in the story, Uncle Alex acted like the caribou when it was caught in a trap.

"His own sons killed the caribou," Petra said. "But they listened when it died so they skinned the dead caribou carefully. They found a man inside and the hunter went home to his family. In the meantime, his mother-in-law had died."

~~~

After Dawn went upstairs with her schoolbooks, Petra said, "Mrs. Helsunk won't think the hat looks right on me."

Young Fen took her hand and tucked her arm under the wing of his. He often reflected at the fire for an hour at a time just as if he were in a boat waiting for fish. "You're the only one that can wear such a hat around here. I'm going to make sure of that. I think I can find out who's doing the poaching," he said.

"I wouldn't wear it if they thought we would kill a swan for a hat."

"They know we wouldn't do that. But if they don't know, they'll find out about the law on poaching. Sheriff Farefax hasn't put any new notices up. The others got torn down somehow. He says all the notices get torn down when he's not lookin'."

"But I'm only wearing the hat on an occasion," Petra said. "I don't think Mrs. Helsunk's is the right occasion."

"It's an occasion to me."

"I wouldn't wear it to your mother's."

Petra didn't often go to the inlet. She found an excuse when Glenda invited her and now it was easier to visit Mrs. Helsunk. Young Fen felt badly about the way they got married even if she didn't mind then. Their wedding in Sitka with just Alex there seemed a sorrow to his parents at first. After Young Fen's argument with his father, he was uncomfortable with them, even when he encountered his father fishing. He said he wasn't ever going back to his father's boat.

In fact, Petra was reminded of the white bird story when she went to the swan migrations. It wasn't uncommon for women to wake up with nothing but two feathers, themselves and their child.

She was nonplussed at possessing the swan pelt, an expense Young Fen wouldn't consider unless something was needed. He put off decisions about the parlor room, mainly because he didn't want to spend the money for furniture that came by ship. He hadn't found a man who could make a carpentered piece since Frances's Paul went to California. Then Petra knew that the old swan meant something as sacred as the church to Young Fen.

Before Petra knew Young Fen, she and Alex went hunting with Jerome, a man who traded with their father Dmitri in Fairbanks. They stayed at Jerome's shack but one night, he told Petra that there was plenty of room for two in his sleeping bag.

"She's got her own," Alex said.

"I thought you natives were hospitable with your women," Jerome said. He was strong in constitution and his desire to learn from Dmitri was what made him a good hunting partner.

Alex was disgusted at him because, after he had some liquor, he turned into another man. "My sister's mournin' our parents. Besides, we never lived in a native village."

Jerome was usually stingy with liquor but that night, he said he'd share it.

"I'm not going to watch you," Alex said when Jerome started playing under Petra's parka. "You already have a wife and child. She's old enough to have one."

When Alex said that, Petra didn't want a child by Jerome. In Fairbanks, he couldn't have two wives. She struggled with him and said, "I'm not some mink in your trap."

"That's what you are. You're a little mink." He pushed her face into his stringy beard and pulled at the tie in her sealskin pants.

"Oh no, I'm a seal," she said, noticing that Alex was getting hold of Jerome's gun. Their father's gun was buried somewhere in the avalanche.

"I've got gold in my pants," Alex said, pointing the gun.

"You're not stealin' my gun!" Jerome yelled. He held on to Petra harder so that Alex might shoot her instead of him. Then he pulled at her pants and threw off her parka right in front of Alex. Jerome dragged Petra to his fur sleeping bag and set her on his lap, still pulling at her pants.

Alex was but fifteen and didn't know what to do at first. Finally he came nearer and sorted them out, attempting to set the gun on Jerome's shoulder. When Jerome grabbed it, Petra got away from him like a seal.

Alex struggled with him and then Petra grabbed the gun while Jerome didn't know which way to point it.

"You're not stealing my gun! I'll tell everyone in Fairbanks about Tuskoffey's son! And that he's got some gold on him too! You'll make some guide, Alex, coming back with the furs and no partner."

When Petra got to the door with the gun, Alex prevented Jerome from assailing her again. Then they both fled the cabin. Petra dropped the gun near a tree so that Jerome would be ashamed. He was the only person Alex could convince to trap with him. They knew he wouldn't hunt them in the woods like animals and that he'd accuse them of stealing his gun everywhere he went.

Since they were afraid of the talk in Fairbanks, they went down to the coast and found a salmon boat. Petra cut her hair off and dressed like a boy.

After Young Fen guessed that Petra was a girl, Alex told him about Jerome and he made it worse than it was, probably so that Young Fen wouldn't like Petra.

Alex said, "I guess we'll have to hunt until we find another fishing boat."

"I'll hunt with you awhile," Young Fen said. "I know the best hunting places around here."

"You won't treat her like a hunting partner," Alex said. "You've been looking at her for being a girl."

They had gotten some brandy from one of the crew on the fishing boat and somehow Young Fen convinced Alex that he wouldn't touch Petra. And he would keep their secrets. Alex was glad of Young Fen's siding with them on the boat. They became a threesome that summer. Young Fen had as little experience with women as Alex.

Even now, Petra was afraid of seeing Jerome because he talked of hunting on Kodiak Island. Of course, many a man going through town looked like him. Yet she thought she saw him on her way to Frances's the other day. If she were wearing the swan bonnet, he'd never think it was her.

The swan bonnet had somehow put away the past. And Young Fen's plans to stop poachers might make up the old argument with his father. He was turning the logs away from the fire now.

"What about Mrs. Helsunk's temperance society?" he wondered. "Do you want to help with it?"

"Liquor can make men into ravenous animals," Petra said. She saw that Young Fen was thinking about something else.

"Mrs. Helsunk might help us to stop the poaching. And she can tell Dawn about them drinking sailors. Wouldn't hurt for Dawn to hear her talk."

"Dawn's been drawing from that catalog again. She's getting to the age where she's noticed around here," Petra said.

"Well, she can't go around in a boy's clothing. She'd be recognized." To think of that made Young Fen smile.

SIXTEEN

On Wednesday, waiting for her mother, Dawn drew with her swan plume. Her hand seemed to float over a sketch done with a pencil that was unevenly sharpened with her father's penknife. The drawing didn't compare to catalog pictures. But her mother's face under the swan hat looked better in the ink of the feather pen.

She even had time to outline the words underneath the drawing: *Last swan bonnet. Made in Alaska from priceless pelt.* Her letters were calm and clear when she used the swan plume at home. At school, Miss Banrath used to say that her letters looked as if they were battling a strong wind. She practiced to make them stand like a tree instead of like a sail.

Dawn wondered if the swan bonnet would make her mother feel more composed when she walked through town.

Her father had coached them on answering people who noticed it. "It'll serve as a decoy. The migration will be in a few weeks. If anyone starts askin' questions about the hat, remember where you were and what they looked like if they're not from around here. Or who they are. Tell them about the old swan. If they ask about migrations, send them to the smokehouse."

Petra was both sullen and excited about this. "Frances might have made one of those feather dusters out of that swan. Reminding every ruffian of their own law is worse than cleaning house," she had replied.

But she didn't look so sullen when she came downstairs, her step as silent as if she were wearing mukluks. She looked serene, better than Dawn's picture of her. Turning only her chin because of the hat ties, Petra said, "Dawn, get your grandmother's shawl on now. Are you sure you want to sit at Mrs. Helsunk's house? You'll have to attend to her and only speak when you're asked to. It's like going to church or to school. Even if it's Saturday."

"I want to see her parlor." Dawn put on her straw hat, adorned now with the swan feather in its band.

"C'mon now." Her mother didn't say again that parlors were not plentiful in their town.

The swan bonnet bobbed just ahead of Dawn until she and her mother were slogging the caked road to the boardwalk. "I'll tell people about the swan hat," Dawn said. "I'll even ask them if they hunt. And remind them about poaching."

Her mother reminded her about talking to sailors. They didn't usually hunt anyway. With the swan bonnet on though, Petra couldn't keep Dawn from swerving around wagon troughs and noticing how the men were watching them.

"You can't chatter with people as if they were your Uncle Alex," her mother was saying. *She* never did. It was a new thing for her to talk at all to the tangly-bearded men in lumberjack jackets, the strange fishermen roving around in slickers, or the sailors in brass-buttoned greatcoats.

"What if people think Uncle Alex gave you the hat?" The thought worried Dawn. Everyone knew where they got their polar bear rug and where Frances obtained polar bear fur. "He's always saying that nature is the law of the north."

"If they know Alex, they would never think he gave me this hat."

Petra almost lurched in another direction when a fisherman leered at her and tooted a call that could carry across a deck. "Hello Missus! That your southwester?"

Calm and glum, Petra merely dodged the man. She sailed through the bluff talk about gold and seals and bear, her eyes shaded by the hat brim. She didn't see what Dawn noted, that the men were actually moving aside for her. There was still the usual cursing cluster standing in the alley past Thaddeus's. Somebody was always flushed and truculent and had a fist like a raring weasel. Another supplanted the air with a swear word.

Dawn observed, "I thought you were going to answer that sailor. And say the hat's a memento."

"Young Fen didn't mean that we should stop outside of Toddy's. His women have mementos too." Petra didn't say what she often said to Dawn once they were past the men: "Malamutes bark with more civility." She smoothed the feathers at her hat brim with her hand and said something new about the men. "I suppose people curse like that when they're unhappy."

"I thought it was ship talk," Dawn said. In the harbor, a ship was sledged like a whale.

"I'm told that they come from places where women won't listen to their cursing," Petra replied. "I want to talk to Frances about these feathers. They hinder me."

They had reached the Snow Clothing Store and her mother went in so quickly that she looked like Bustle gliding.

~~~

The counter at Snow Clothing put the width of a plank walk between Frances and a stout customer standing inside. Waiting to talk with Frances, Petra said, "I think it's better to show up late at Mrs. Helsunk's than before she's ready for us. I guess I don't want to stand in the smokehouse with this hat on."

They might have sauntered along the ocean where the waves shaved up from the deep and where the fishermen her mother knew would be as puzzled as Toddy at the hat. Bustle's feathers would be near the water and her mother might feel as calm as she looked. If a sailor followed them, they could lead him straight to the smokehouse. Her mother wasn't usually so exact about time. Now she shambled over to a stack of woolen caps but the swan hat, sweeping past the stout bearded man, caused him to gape.

Frances said to him, "I expect your parka will be ready in three weeks, Mr. Marmont."

Instead of replying to Frances, he addressed Petra. "Is that an Alaska swan your hat is made from?"

Petra grimaced, begrudging him conversation at first.

Dawn informed him, "Alaska swans turn into United States swans when they migrate."

"He knows that, Dawn," her mother said.

"But they land 'round here, about this time of the year, don't they?" The man squinted and his face turned pulpy.

"They pass through," Petra said.

"But someone shot that swan," the man bluffed.

Frances answered him. "It's not lawful anymore to hunt swan. Nobody can shoot swan around here. Even if Alaska's not a state."

Mr. Marmont's eyes gleamed impudently at the swan bonnet. Dawn strived to keep quiet while her mother struggled to tell the man about the keepsake. Usually, she would gesture to Dawn and they would slip out of the shop.

Mr. Marmont might have been forewarned of that because he walked towards the door and gripped the door handle. He opened it only enough for a breeze to come in and swish a few feathers on the swan hat. As he opened the door wider, he made sure that his bulk was blocking passage. The feathers riffled as if the hat wanted to fly away. Staring at the hat, he said to Frances, "If I'm out of town when the jacket's done, you can leave word at Toddy's."

Finally, Petra said in a severe way, "This hat was made from an old sick swan, not a migrating swan."

Mr. Marmont let the door close.

"It nested for more than twenty years near here. It warn't hunted before it died. This swan hat is a relic, Mr. Marmont, and a family memento."

"It died of old age?"

"It did!" Frances said.

Mr. Marmont jeered, incredulous. Disappointed and put off, he banged the door as he left Snow Clothing.

"Well. His tune was easy to tell. That hat *is* a decoy," Frances said. "He looked about ready to go swan hunting."

Dawn found this a triumph. "If Grandma Glenda hears gunshots, we'll look for Mr. Marmont. I could stay out at the inlet and watch for him and anyone else who's curious about the hat." It wasn't enough to inform everyone who asked about the hat. She was ready to ride the shore of the bay to stop any hunters and to keep the swan flocks from dwindling.

"You'll have school then. Young Fen is prepared to be a vigilante," her mother said. "I don't think you'd want to be there if Mr. Marmont or other poachers are around." She gave her head a sharp shake, looking up at the hat brim. "Frances, this hat is a trial to wear. You saw what happened in church. It's a beautiful hat. But the feathers at the brim prevent me from seeing where a man like Mr. Marmont is going. I don't like to look right at someone like him. Maybe it should be altered."

Dawn protested, "But he stood off like he would with a swan. I could see that some were admiring it."

Her mother's dark eyes looked as grim as a swan's. It was as if she were turning into one like the swan people in the native story Uncle Alex told. Usually, migrations were like the story. The swans went away and left the two feathers. Bustle left her whole pelt for them. She might have gone to her old nesting place to die.

"Swans don't have feathers near their faces," her mother said. "You were right happy about your hat feather being in the place of a ribbon. It doesn't hinder you there."

Frances bobbed around Dawn's mother, inspecting the hat. Then she soothed, "You're just not used to wearing a dress hat, Petra. A woman can't act as if she's got much to do when she's wearing a trimmed hat. And you can pretend you don't see someone like Mr. Marmont."

Dawn added, "He didn't ask about anything else but the hat." She would rather hear him ask about leggings or where a man could have his hair cut than about swans.

Petra admitted, "It might feel like a burden today because we're on our way to Mrs. Helsunk's."

SEVENTEEN

The Helsunk's house could be discovered by any stray sailor wandering about the harbor town. The plank walk in front was swept, there was a tiller on the front door, and "Helsunk" was painted on the frosty house as if it were a ship's prow. On the second floor was a porch and balustrade from where Captain Helsunk looked out to sea with his spyglass.

Petra was relieved to arrive at the house. Near the General Store, she received nothing but awed ogling. The men kept to their space though and even moved to the store's veranda, looking as if a swan had floated to shore. A fisherman who knew Petra stepped back as if he had seen a beluga whale surface and said, "Is that you, Petra? When did you come by that hat?"

Dawn stared at the Helsunk's curtains, tied inside the windows like complicated hair arrangements. Her mother stood before the front door, checked her hat ties, but then she sighed. When she rapped on the door, it seemed as heavy as a block of ice. And the tiller rattled, wheeling a little, which made her jump back. Dawn grasped the tiller, afraid that it would fall from the door, and then it rolled into a notch. A bell jingled on the other side of the door.

Soon Mrs. Helsunk was inspecting them through her chained spectacles. She had another maroon dress on, this one with blue braid on it, and its skirt looked as stiff as her umbrella.

"Come in Petra and, ah, Dawn," she said, peering at Dawn's best blue and gray jumper under the blue wool shawl. "You're a little late. Did you stand here long before you figured out this bell rigging?"

"Dawn figured it out. All I know about is nets and ropes," Petra said, stepping onto a clipped grizzly rug that was cut into a perfect rectangle for Mrs. Helsunk's entryway. She began to sway on it, untying the swan bonnet.

But Mrs. Helsunk seemed to be barring the way into the town's only parlor, she was so plump. Dawn narrowed her eyes at wallpaper the color of gentians as Mrs. Helsunk said, "You can wear that lovely hat into the parlor, Petra. You'll never guess where I got the boot-wipe from, wholesale."

After Mrs. Helsunk said *boot-wipe*, Petra looked at the sensible shape that Frances cut although she didn't find it remarkable that Uncle Alex sold it to Mrs. Helsunk. Then she and Dawn both swiped over it until every bit of town mud was off of their boots.

"We could take our boots off," Petra offered. She was staring at a carpet covered with petals in the parlor room.

"Take off your boots!" Mrs. Helsunk said and sniffed. "Young women in the States are exhibiting their ankles and even their legs. No, Petra, tread on it as if it were moss." Then Mrs. Helsunk took Dawn's straw hat because Dawn had taken it off to see everything better. Still, she faltered on the carpet that was like a framed picture, thinking of moss and wildflowers and how she didn't usually trample flowers.

A soft upholstered sofa was in the room beside a low table so shiny that it looked like a huge tray filled with water. At one end of the table was a captain's chair. Opposite that, a polished mantle supported scrimshaw figurines, jade oddities, and vases of silver that made reflections in a mirror. There was a brass-faced clock in a cabinet so tall that Dawn had to bend backwards to see the time on it.

Mrs. Helsunk excused herself from the room while Petra walked off of the carpet to examine the wallpaper. Pulling at the ties of her hat again, she said, "Look Dawn. There are conches on the walls."

Dawn stepped backwards from the towering clock and tripped into a spindly chair that was beside a roll top desk. The chair was so light and carved that it toppled, but Dawn and her mother rescued it. During this, the swan bonnet slipped off of Petra's head and landed on the carpet near the mantel. Mrs. Helsunk came tinkling in with a tray just in time to see the hat gliding.

"My goodness, Petra! Can't you keep that hat on?"

Dawn hastened across the carpet and collected the swan bonnet. Its feathers felt gentle on her hands, which were as nervous as if she had a pan of gold in them.

"You'd think it still had a spirit to fly!" Petra said, also miffed. At least her hair was pinned up except for one straying tassel.

"Nonsense," Mrs. Helsunk replied. She set the tray down to show them the ring of cake on it. It looked like snow-peaked ranges of mountains with its icing drizzling down the sides.

Dawn had just determined to keep the hat near her during the visit when Mrs. Helsunk prodded her, "Aren't you going to give your mother her hat? To keep her hair in place? You're not superstitious, are you?"

Dawn trod over the floor flowers and handed the hat to her mother.

"I don't think I can eat with the hat on," Petra said.

"You should try to," Mrs. Helsunk coaxed until Petra fixed it back onto her head. Then Mrs. Helsunk swept into the next room where she made more tinkling with cups and saucers.

Petra made a neat bow with the leather bonnet ties in front of the clear mirror. Then she sat on a stuffed chair that had ferns stitched on it. When she leaned back, she knew the swan feathers might get bent so she sat on the edge of the chair with her back straight. Dawn settled into the captain's chair where she could steady herself at the armrests.

When Mrs. Helsunk jingled in, she said edgily, "Move over to the sofa, Petra. And Dawn, I'll have you sit on this chair." She set down the tray and hoisted the lightweight desk chair to the coffee table. When Dawn had given up the captain's chair, Mrs. Helsunk heaved herself onto the ferny chair.

"The captain wouldn't want to see a girl in a man's seat," Mrs. Helsunk said, eyeing Petra. "He might come in for a biscuit. Parlor guests get situated in chairs like ship passengers. But how could anyone know what society does around here?"

Dawn glanced at her mother. The bow at her chin looked cheerful and it kept her from having any expression except an amiable smirk.

Not having to eat with a hat on, Dawn balked at the sliver Mrs. Helsunk cut for her from the cake with mountain ranges. That would be a mistake at her house. Besides that, what Mrs. Helsunk was saying made her fingers grip the shawl her grandmother knit for her.

"Is there another old swan at the inlet? The mate of the one that died?"

Dawn answered while Petra took a fork from Mrs. Helsunk. "Her mate didn't come back this spring."

"That's a shame," Mrs. Helsunk said, but she seemed more let down than sad.

"They think there might have been poachers at the bay," Dawn said, taking a fork from Mrs. Helsunk.

"That too? Well, there's another reason why townsfolk need to help our sheriff. A temperance society, that's what other towns have."

Her mother was looking down at her cake as if she were ice fishing.

~~~

"Dawn, the milk is for you. Do you drink coffee already?" Mrs. Helsunk frowned at Petra. "I guess you know, Petra, what sort of malcontents come up here. Mangy boys without much of an upbringing. Many have no home 'back home' at all."

"Boys looking for a living from fur or mining," Petra replied.

Dawn was surprised that her mother didn't show her dislike for the scanty-bearded strangers who asked for advice about Snow Clothing and accommodations. "Doesn't the ocean slop all over them before they get here?" Dawn heard her own voice sounding timid. When Mrs. Helsunk didn't seem to hear her, she swallowed some milk. In her nervousness, she had eaten her whole sliver of cake.

"My, you're hungry." Mrs. Helsunk cut another sliver of cake for Dawn. "Of course I've only been on Captain Helsunk's ship. We came with our mother to join our father after the gold rush. Since my wedding, I've only taken one trip with Captain Helsunk. Down to San Francisco. He hasn't been able to get me out in a fishing skiff since!" Mrs. Helsunk's eyes glistened at Petra.

Petra had to sit so stiffly in the swan hat that her coffee spilled onto her saucer during its route to her mouth.

"A napkin, Petra. A napkin," Mrs. Helsunk commanded. "Make a square with the cup, up and then transport it level to your lips. Now, I saw the young men when they boarded the ship. They were rogues. It was 1917, two years before Prohibition. Every one of them tried to bring bottles on board. And Captain Helsunk was known for keeping a sober ship! They were boys like those out in the salmon dinghies, Petra."

Petra sipped her coffee, her head stretched up like a swan's. Dawn had wondered what went on in parlors. It might be nice, she speculated, if Mrs. Helsunk weren't there.   The food and the cushions and the moss-soft carpet put her into a trance. It was how she felt when she watched the summer's feathered sea foam come again and again to the shore. And her mother was like a swan sedate on the waves.

Mrs. Helsunk opened a napkin onto her lap and spoke. "I keep telling the captain when he misses his voyages that sailors would be drinking in every foreign port.   He swears that he could change the drunken tread of a sailor into a dance with the high seas. Speaking of dancing, Petra, I saw a Russian ballet when I was in San Francisco. My, they used a lot of swan feathers for the costumes. A good thing, too. They'd make your bonnet look like a mere swatch. They could still hunt them then. But the saloons were beginning to close at an earlier curfew. I tell you, when we left the concert hall, I saw men banging on saloon doors for a drink! Petra, do you know what happens when they do that here? In this town?"

Despite her manners, Mrs. Helsunk's face looked apoplectic, the purple of her walls. She began wiping her finicky fingers in her napkin. "There are ship's biscuits there. And strawberry jam!" Mrs. Helsunk seemed to shout at Dawn, her chin wobbling like a seal's. "Fresh from our strawberry patch. Do you know what happens, Petra, when those boys want a drink?"

"They find it," Petra said. Unlike Mrs. Helsunk, she said this with the flared repose of her hat feathers.

"That's right, Petra.   Under the sign of 'Eatery', at the mining office, in the cannery, at the cabins, under bobsled blankets, in native dwellings, on boat bottoms. And I hope not in the smokehouse."

Too calmly, Petra said, "They say the sheriff wants to close the saloons and drink his beer too."

"My brother, Sheriff Farefax, closed the saloons.   He will be speaking at the temperance meeting. Deputy Shamison, who keeps them closed, will be there too. And Minister Calvert will be there. I can count on you and Young Fen then, Petra? Captain Helsunk will tell how he kept a temperate ship."

Mrs. Helsunk put a ship's biscuit on Dawn's plate and then she put one on Petra's. "You must be warm," she said. She leaned around Petra to open the window behind the sofa. After it came open a wedge, she hung at the swan hat and even touched the hat's brim.

"Maybe we'll come to the meeting," Petra said. "This is only a wild territory. But the States forgot what happened when they tried to stop drinking here before. My father told me about it before he died in a tragic accident and left Alex and me homeless." She lurched away from Mrs. Helsunk, stood, and stepped around the tinkling table. Then she checked her hat ties in front of the gilded mirror. "I think I'll take off my bonnet," she said.

"But I want the captain to see it," Mrs. Helsunk protested. "Now, tell me about the deceased Mr. Tuskoffey."

"About when the United States Army abolished drinking in Alaska," Petra said. "*They* failed to abolish it. Before them, the Russians prohibited drinking here. And they failed to stop it too." Petra paced away from the mirror and then when she turned, she blinked as if she were balked at her own feathery head. "After the gold rushes started, the saloons all opened up again. You wouldn't have wanted to see the boys then."

When Petra gave Mrs. Helsunk a wary glance, Mrs. Helsunk told her the time and place of the temperance meeting.

EIGHTEEN

Dawn expected that her mother was standing because it was time to leave. But then the feathers of her hat swirled like sea spray as Captain Helsunk blew into the parlor.

"Bergs ahead!" he exclaimed. "There's that swan hat! How'd you get that headful of swan?"

Petra sat down on the sofa again, her smile gone mute. She looked at Mrs. Helsunk while the captain's eyes gleamed as brusquely as hailstones.

Mrs. Helsunk was eager to answer him. "Petra has a quaint story, Captain, about an old swan at Fen O'Raine's bay. She says it died of old age."

Captain Helsunk, in the captain's chair, reached for a ship's biscuit. "Aye, that's a good one!" he said, an icy eye winking. "Fen gave her an Irish nudge with his shotgun!"

"My Grandpa Fen doesn't shoot swans!" Dawn protested. "My grandmother was there. She heard a swansong."

"Aye, and she saw it swooned like a white snake in the grass," Captain Helsunk said with an awful glee.

"She fed it. It fed in her garden when it was feeble," Dawn said.

Then Petra said, "I'd take heed of that story before I'd believe one from a sailor's mouth."

Dawn noticed how the eyes of Captain and Mrs. Helsunk met. She turned to her mother and saw with horror that the feathers of her hat were flexing upward and shuddering around the back of her head.

Captain Helsunk put down his plate while Mrs. Helsunk turned purple again. The swan bonnet's feathers were wavering like the Northern Lights.

Not knowing this, Petra said, "Captain Helsunk, have you ever seen Fen O'Raine or his wife sell a swan pelt?"

Chuckling, Captain Helsunk's eyes dipped out of view and back again.

"Petra, your hat," Mrs. Helsunk said.

"Yes, I know they were going to sell this swanskin," Petra said.

Dawn informed her, "The hat feathers are bending up!"

"Why, they're standing on end almost like the quills on the native fishing visors!" Mrs. Helsunk exclaimed.

"Those hats are made with sea lion whiskers," Captain Helsunk corrected her.

Petra's hand swished through the spray of plumes. The captain began making oaths about sleets and sails while Petra leapt up and made her way to the mirror again. The back brim of the bonnet had crimped upwards. Once it was coaxed back into place, the feathers interlaced again in their tranquil dovetail.

Mrs. Helsunk closed the window behind the sofa.

"A gust in the porthole," the captain said.

"I don't mean to wear this hat often," Petra said in a new sedate parlor voice.

"You must wear it to our meeting," Mrs. Helsunk decided. "If you want to tell what you learned from the deceased Mr. Tuskoffey, everyone will listen."

"Mrs. Helsunk, this hat won't quit being a swan," Petra said.

Dawn added, "It ruffled up when she was talking to a hunter today."

"By the same reasoning, your polar bear hat made you lumber, Petra." Mrs. Helsunk stood up and threw her head back. "My dear, there are girls who are made to walk around with books on their heads so they have the dignity to wear hats like that. You're not used to it. Poor Frances hasn't had much of a chance at doing dress hats. You'd better wear that hat to the meeting. If you think it's possessed with a swan spirit or some such superstition, Minister Calvert will be there." She stood in her stiff ruffles near the coffee pot. "Here's your cup of coffee, Captain. How are the ship's biscuits? I pounded them with a mallet for ten minutes." Then Mrs. Helsunk paraded to Captain Helsunk with the cup and saucer, remaining at attention beside him so that Dawn felt she should stand too.

Her mother stayed still on the carpet. "We ought to be going now, Dawn," she said.

As Mrs. Helsunk accompanied Petra to the hallway, she made her promise to wear the swan bonnet to the temperance meeting.

"Dawn, is it?" Captain Helsunk detained her.

"Yes."

The captain's eyes glinted. "I'll bet you watch fleets of swans at that port of your grandfather's."

"If there isn't school."

"I've spied the swans overhead! About the first week of October? When I saw a migrating bird from my ship, I took it as a sign of a snug cargo and good weather," the captain said jovially. "So, the first week of October? Now I take that sight as the sign of a hard winter beginning up north."

Only husky dogs had such wintry eyes as the captain's. They probably chilled sailors. Maybe Captain Helsunk had been suspicious of Grandpa Fen because the captain was in the habit of being suspicious.

"The swans don't always come the same week. Winter doesn't come the same week every year."

"A whole fleet of swans comes through sometimes," Captain Helsunk said. His eyes gazed out at his lawn as if there were restful waves there.

"Every year the fleet is smaller," Dawn informed him.

"I suppose it looks that way to you," Captain Helsunk replied. "Mrs. Helsunk is always telling me that I remember my years at sea as grander than they were."

"Dawn!" came her mother's call.

Dawn gladly trod across the carpet to collect her straw hat and say goodbye to Mrs. Helsunk in the hallway. Once the thick door was shut, she paced ahead to the boardwalk. But her mother must have known that two heads were watching her at the bay window because she walked with a slow glide.

"It's one thing to have manners, Dawn," she said when they were on the boardwalk. "And it's another thing to know something. People like Mrs. Helsunk change their ideas, even their laws, as if they were clothing fashions. But I don't think they can tell me what to wear and when to wear it. When I was a girl, there were schools for natives and schools for settlers. Alex and I were neither and both. That's why your uncle is so insolent. He can tell when a rule depends on what you say or what you can pay."

They were waiting at a corner for a wagon to pass. With her eyes shaded, Petra didn't see that a man in a red and black logging jacket was contemplating the swan bonnet. Sidling up, he said, "Ma'am, is your hat made from a trumpeter or a whistler swan?"

Still indignant at Mrs. Helsunk, Petra answered, "I should know that it was a whistler because the swan nested near here and died a natural death."

"Pardon, I don't know these parts. Or which swans nest here." The man's voice was clenched as if he were prying open a tin can. "I want to get up to Anchorage along the waterways. I'm looking for a logging camp thereabouts. You must know your way through the foothills if you know about nestin' swans."

"Go on," Dawn's mother said shortly. "Go on over to that smokehouse there and ask my husband."

Because her mother reduced the quaint story about the swan to her usual brief reply, Dawn added, "If you tell us your name, we can get you a guide."

But the man only took one last look at the swan hat and strode in the direction of the General Store.

"It's not lawful to shoot swans here!" Dawn shouted after him.

Her mother chided, "Dawn, never call after men on the road. Do you know what Mrs. Helsunk said in the hall? She said, 'It's not so hard to wear a swan bonnet to please your husband. Mine makes me pound out biscuit dough with a mallet that came from a ship's kitchen.' That woman with a parlor can't do things the way she wants to in her own kitchen. She has things no better. You know what I said to her? I asked her to bring a plate of ship's biscuits to the temperance meeting."

Between remarks about the hat from other rovers, Dawn wondered, "If we have a parlor, will Mrs. Helsunk come over instead of Uncle Alex?"

"I don't think she would," her mother replied. "Frances might come over more often. But she'll probably bring her knitting in the basket I wove for her."

~~~

On the Wednesday of the temperance meeting, Dawn and her father sat at the hearth in their social clothing. Dawn's mother was upstairs putting on the swan bonnet. Smoked salmon, cabbage soup, and potato bread were ready in the kitchen for the potluck.

Taking Dawn's straw hat from the hearth table, her father said, "You don't mind wearing your lucky feathers, do you?" He often had a lucky swan feather in his jacket pocket.

"No one asks about them. At school, they might think we couldn't get any ribbon."

They both glanced up at the ceiling and her father remarked, "I guess you're right about that swan bonnet hindering your mother. She's never kept us waitin' like this. What if she can't bring herself to wear it again? Here, show me that list of inquirers from when she wore it in town."

Dawn retrieved a piece of paper from her tablet. But her father only muttered over it, his mutton chops set forward on his jaw.

Dawn warned him, "She says she can't see who's coming with the feathers on the sides of her eyes. But most people stand away when they see the hat."

"Dress hats and clothing inhibit a person. We can tell the people at the meeting about it." Her father shook his head over the words she copied with her swan plume:

Mr. Marmont. Red and black checkered jacket. Black beard. At Snow Clothing.
Man in sailor boots and jacket at General Store. Yellow hair and brown beard.
Man in elk skin jacket. Brown beard.
Fisherman by the name of Fred. Black sweater. Brown hair and orange beard.
Captain Helsunk.
Man in red and black jacket. Sent to smokehouse.
Man outside Thaddeus's. Western boots and leather jacket. Black whiskers.
Man in hide jacket and Snow Clothing hunting hat. Brown beard.

"That's eight people in one afternoon askin' about swans. Well, tell me if you recognize any of them at the meeting."

"They were asking about swan migrations too. The best way to get their names is by standing in the Snow Clothing store. Then Frances knows who they are."

"I don't know about that. It wouldn't hurt your mother to wear the hat when she goes to the General Store. Reynolds knows names there too. Well, at least the logger was warned at the smokehouse."

"I don't think Captain Helsunk believed Bustle was that old," Dawn said.

"I don't want those men shootin' swans any more than Mrs. Helsunk wants them sneakin' bottles. The last thing the sheriff thinks about is swans," her father replied.

Coming into the room, Petra said, "I guess he'll think about them tonight." Her step was as light as Reindog's toenails. "This hat should get attention for your announcement about poaching. And the whole town will know that I'm innocent in wearing it. It's a special occasion." She went to the kitchen and began lugging the soup pan, wrapped in a blanket, to the hall.

"I'll take the soup," Dawn's father said. "You can remind people about poaching when you tell about the early days of the territory. When they tried to stop the drinking."

"They didn't do anything about the swans then," Petra objected. "The natives didn't take too many of them. Aleut Jon's mother is coming, isn't she?"

"She's going. She's worried because she knows of someone who's got a still."

"There's some who will come just to look like they don't know about any still. That's like us saying we don't know about swans."

As Young Fen motioned for Dawn to carry the platter of potato bread, she said, "Grandma Glenda says she doesn't know what's happened to the trumpeter swans."

Her mother carried the wrapped parcels of salmon in her arms. Dawn sat in the back of the wagon, holding onto the soup pan. From outside of Toddy's, people stared at the fluttering swan hat as they drove to the schoolhouse.

NINETEEN

In the schoolroom, adults were sitting on the benches. Miss Banrath directed Dawn and her parents to the adjoining room where they could set their food on the large table there. Miss Banrath was wearing her new wool jacket and skirt but after everyone was settled, she sat down near Minister Calvert and his wife.

Then Mrs. Helsunk gave a speech about Prohibition and the many arrests that Deputy Shamison made in the past years. After she told about Captain Helsunk's temperate ship, the deputy stood up, saying he couldn't stay long, but that was because he and Sheriff Farefax were overcome with the responsibilities of running the town. They had a man in jail that was wanted for robbery in Fairbanks. Then the deputy told how he had spent whole evenings following the trail of fermented wine and the bottles that came by boat.

"Excuse me, Miss Banrath and Minister Calvert," Deputy Shamison said, "but I have ta tell you about some of the havoc alcohol has caused around here. One of these stills I found, I couldn't tell which man ran it 'cause two got into a fight over the money box. That still made them so drunk that they both admitted their guilt, admitted it as they wrastled over the money they made from it. I had ta find that money box too and I'm lucky to be here to tell you that they were charging so much for their alcohol that you'd think it was the water in the Fountain of Youth! An' then, up in the rooms at Toddy's, there was a sailor sellin' bottles from a ship. Them ships stop in Vancouver and all the crew buy British whiskey. Well, he had a woman in the room with him when I found him an' she didn't want me touchin' the drawer with her underthings! She said I was after something else, only because I had to get a corset out of the drawer to find a bottle."

"Deputy Shamison!" Mrs. Helsunk interrupted. "Children, you should now go into the other room where you can eat together. Miss Banrath will be teaching you about temperance."

Most of the young folks at the meeting were more than ten-years-old. But they were used to doing their schoolwork in the adjacent room when Miss Banrath taught the younger ones to read. Mrs. Shamison and Frances were there, arranging the potluck dishes.

"I thought everyone would get their food in here," Mrs. Shamison said. "I guess we'll have to bring it out to the teacher's desk after the first speeches."

"It'd be too crowded anyway," Frances said. "I'll help you."

They began moving the dishes to one end of the table while Frances told Mrs. Shamison how she made the swan bonnet. Dawn and her schoolmate Clara Ann helped and then they both filled their tin plates with sourdough bread, cloudberry spread, rabbit stew, and moose meat. Soon they were seated with Davy Shamison, the storekeeper's daughters, and Kenny, Smokehouse Jon's boy. When Frances told about the swan feathers flaring into her face, Davy flipped a fresh cloudberry into his mouth with his fork. He flipped another and missed, causing the Reynolds girls to giggle.

Dawn wondered if her mother would eat with the hat on. She said to Clara Ann, "Mrs. Helsunk wanted my mother to wear the swan hat to the meeting." But that made the Reynolds girls giggle all the more. Davy was smirking at her. When Dawn wore a swan feather in her straw hat, it didn't cause a sensation.

"I forget that it's Petra wearing that hat," Mrs. Shamison was saying. "I haven't seen anything so genteel since I was a girl in Missouri. And they say it was made from an old swan at Glenda O'Raine's."

Loud laughter from the schoolroom muffled Frances's reply. Then she and Mrs. Shamison began carrying the pans of food to the schoolroom. The schoolroom quieted the way it did when Miss Banrath entered it. Dawn heard Davy saying to Kenny, "Easy to break its neck without shooting a gun. I guess that's not huntin'."

"You've never been near a swan, I guess," Kenny said, his glossy hair falling over one eye. "If it was alive, its wings would knock you off your feet."

"The hat was made from a decrepit swan," Davy said. "Anyone could say they rescued a swan from a wolverine without ever puttin' a bullet in it."

Dawn protested, "My grandfather didn't make up such a story."

"Swans are stronger than you think," Kenny maintained. "If it was so weak, it'd be in the water."

"You could hardly get near a swan, Davy," Dawn said. "And if you could because it was used to you, you wouldn't do such an awful thing."

Dawn turned to Clara Ann, sitting next to her. Clara Ann often wondered if Davy didn't tell tales too tall for his height. The way he told things, he would have had to be along with his father, the deputy sheriff. Davy must have taken time off from school to search out liquor stills and chase after pirates who stole from gold prospectors. He described in detail scar-producing brawls that must have happened late on a school night and at Toddy's when the food tables were used for card games.

"I wouldn't do something awful like that. There are some who would," Davy said. "I'd like to see the migration that's coming up. Last time I saw swans, they were flyin' up the mountain. They must have been in the foothills that day. If I'd had a colt then, I could've spurred it and maybe seen the last ones take off into the air." Davy was talking to Dawn, his eyes cobalt with cheer.

"So long as you didn't have a gun with you," Dawn said. Davy was like her Uncle Alex with his gold nugget. This year, he tantalized other boys with the colt his father bought in Anchorage. It was especially fine, bred from a horse that could overtake most outlaws' horses, he said.

Placidly, Kenny said to Davy, "It must've been a full moon when you saw swans flying."

"No, it warn't," Davy said, obstinate. "It was during the alpenglow."

"They must've been scared up because swans travel at night," Kenny said.

"Might have been," Davy said, and then he eyed Dawn.

At this, Dawn refrained from giving Davy attention. Her Uncle Alex's stories about polar bear brigades were more believable than what Davy claimed. She had never seen both alpenglow and swans flying in formation at the same time, a sight more remarkable than she could tell. But he said he'd seen other uncommon things like a mountain goat spiking a man off a steep ridge. According to Davy, mountain goats and mountain rams could smell when a man had a fight in him. They were almost as effective as Sheriff Farefax.

Dawn noticed a plate of ship's biscuits that Mrs. Shamison left in the room. No one had touched them. Clara Ann was spreading Mrs. Helsunk's strawberry preserves on potato bread. Kenny had pitched himself on the floor with his plate.

Clara Ann was saying, "My mother was practically in a swoon after she saw your mother in the swan hat. I didn't think it was all that different from the polar bear hat that she wears in the winter." Then she munched on the potato bread, mulling this over.

Clara Ann's parents were newcomers as were most of the parents of the girls at school. Some of them stayed only a short time before moving to Anchorage or Fairbanks. Clara Ann's father was working on the railroad that would take them there. Until Clara Ann told Dawn about her ship voyage from Oregon, she had not seemed to come ashore. It was surprising to her that Dawn's mother had native blood. Dawn had found that the newcomer children were not always from one sort of people, either. After she told Clara Ann that besides being Aleut, she was also Irish and Russian, Clara Ann told her what her family was before they were American. "I guess we're nobodies too. My dad says we're Scotch and Irish and my mother says we're Danish and Lutheran too. But here, we're not any of those things."

Now Clara Ann said, "My mother was in a swoon that forgot the other swoon after she crossed the street in front of Captain Helsunk and his motorcar. She says that someday, we'll have one too. Lots of people will."

"Someday will be next year for us," Davy declared.

Clara Ann asked him, "Did you ever ride in the motorcar? I saw your father riding in it."

"When I rode, I wasn't recognizable because of the automobile goggles I had to wear," Davy blustered. "And then there was the time I stowed on the motorcar. I sneaked onto the running board and hung on. It was just like dog sledding. Captain Helsunk didn't see me until we got onto the section near the railroad that's goin' to have to be widened for motorcars. We bounded like reindeer."

Even though Dawn was relieved that the subject had turned from swans, she supposed that Davy was telling another tall tale. She had never seen him in or on Captain Helsunk's motorcar. Ignoring him, she asked Clara Ann, "Did you eat ship's biscuits when you were on the ocean?" There was one thing Dawn knew for sure about Davy. He had never taken an ocean voyage.

"Not many. We were supposed to nibble on them so we wouldn't get seasick. They're dry and gritty, at least on the ship they were." Clara Ann mused at Mrs. Helsunk's biscuits.

"Mrs. Helsunk pounds her biscuits with a mallet from a ship," Dawn said.

Davy boasted, "I've eaten hundreds of ship's biscuits, I guess. Down at the harbor with Pa. Anyone planning to stow on a ship to Sitka has got to get used to them."

"Show us how you stowed without Captain Helsunk seeing you," Kenny said, squinting at Davy from the floor. "Stow a ride on that motorcar tonight."

"First, eat some ship's biscuits," Dawn said. She got up and walked stiffly with the plate of ship's biscuits, the way Mrs. Helsunk did, and put them by Davy's plate.

Putting off an answer about stowing, Davy lavished a ship's biscuit with strawberry preserves. He gulped it with indifferent chews. That and a wave of guffaws from the schoolroom kept him from making any promises about Captain Helsunk's motorcar.

"So, are you going to stow on the captain's motorcar?" Kenny asked again, his eyes glinting like the crack in the doorway.

Davy spluttered after he swallowed a second biscuit. It was Kenny who should try to stow with the captain, he decided. Though Davy had alighted onto the running board of the captain's motorcar as noiselessly as a flea on a sled dog, he had been discovered. But he still got to ride down to the railroad property and back. All Kenny had to do was hide in the bushes, sly Indian that he was and dark as it was getting outside, and as soon as the captain had the motorcar puffing, make a jump for the running board.

It was a feat, Davy admitted. Captain Helsunk was at the meeting because of his ability to spot liquor bottles that sailors tried to stow on board ship. There was a sailor who said he was so religious that he could pray a ship from breaking on the rocks. But his eyes were so bad that he could mistake a whale for land. Besides this, he had an ailment that required a shot glass of mineral oil a day. He also claimed to be the best biscuit-maker and bottle washer on the Pacific.

As if he had been there watching, Davy showed how Captain Helsunk seized the sailor's huge Bible with big print and his brown jugs of oil and his gallon of spring water for his special recipe of Colorado spring water biscuits. In all of those things, the captain found liquor. He said he simply saw the bottles in the sailor's eyeballs, Davy explained.

"If you're goin' to stow, you'd better sneak out right now and crouch in the bushes near the motorcar," Davy said to Kenny. "Captain Helsunk might have noticed that your grandmother is at the meeting but your father ain't. We'll tell your grandma that you went on home. Even if the captain catches you, he'd probably give you a ride home so he can have a word with your father."

Davy shut up because Mrs. Shamison was approaching from the schoolroom.

"Why, I've never seen anything so ill-timed. Funny, Frances, how that hat wants to fly off." And then Mrs. Shamison said more loudly, "A good potluck, isn't it?"

Kenny stared from Davy to Dawn. But he didn't get up from the floor. He only said, "My grandmother probably didn't think it was much like an Aleut potlatch." His dark eyes stayed on Dawn because she had never been to those native gatherings.

"If you want to fill your plates again, you young'uns can come out into the schoolroom now," Mrs. Shamison said. "And Davy, don't you go running off. We're bringing Mrs. Helsunk to her house and need you to carry the stew pan and her coffee pot." She turned to Frances. "There hasn't been a woman or a young'un on the seat of that motorcar since the first day the captain cranked it up."

TWENTY

Their wagon followed the motorcar that contained Captain Helsunk and Mr. Reynolds until it turned towards the harbor to shine headlights on any men there. That kept Dawn thinking of Davy's impish face. His stories weren't the stories of Uncle Alex or Deputy Shamison, stories people often wished weren't real. Davy was so good at bluffing that maybe he *was* at Toddy's during the card games. Maybe Davy did stow on the motorcar and his mother didn't know about it. Swans could get scared up while the sun still shone and alpenglow colored the mountains.

When they got inside their house, Petra said, "I don't think I'll wear this hat for a long time, Fen. I felt like a fool." She stood in the hall and announced, "I don't know about having any parlor for townspeople to come for a sit. They sat and stared tonight and they didn't talk to me about anything except the hat."

Young Fen's mutton chops rippled either because he was ruminating or striving not to laugh. He looked towards the floor, taking off his coat.

"Clara Ann didn't think the swan hat was much different than your polar bear hat," Dawn said.

Her father started towards the hearth to light a fire. "Clara Ann's mother didn't say that. I guess feathers are different from fur. And those people didn't seem very distressed at what I told them about swans, that there aren't any trumpeter swans anymore. They resented our relic. It's what I suspected. Well, I didn't know what to do with that swan pelt except that I didn't want to sell it for export. As if we're in business to do that here."

Petra snatched off the swan bonnet. "You stood up and had your say. And the hat had its say. Your mother knew the best thing to do with a swan pelt, Fen. She would have plucked it and sold it as feathers and down." She took the swan bonnet to the hall cupboard, shaking her head, and then she headed for the stairway. "At least I did my part, telling them the awful truth about drinking people trying to stop drinking in this territory. You'd think those people would know about something so poisonous. But that just stirred 'em up. All that talk about needing a shotgun to bust a poacher. I don't think they even listened to me."

Young Fen showed the green of his eyes. "There's aspiring and envy and coveting that's in towns, Petra. Besides plenty of argument. When I got up to talk about swans, I could feel it backfiring. I was reminding some that the swans are coming in and that they are a scarce luxury."

Petra bounded up the stairs, shaking her hair down from its pins.

Dawn's father kept grumbling. "And then Deputy Shamison asked how was he to tell that our swanskin hadn't been poached. There's always some story, he said. You know what to say to such talk, don't you, Dawn? You tell them about Bustle."

"Sure," Dawn said. But she was guessing that the swan feathers might have flared up again as they did at Mrs. Helsunk's. Her mother was so firm about not wearing it. "What did the hat do?"

"What did the hat do?" Her father gave her a testy look. "Oh, your mother said the hat had its say. But then she can't talk so heatedly when she's wearing it." He glanced at the ceiling where footfalls were subsiding. He didn't seem very insulted about the hat being put away in the cupboard.

"But what did it do this time?" Dawn persisted.

"Well, it made people laugh. Your mother got goin' on vodka and its forbiddance and then whiskey and its forbiddance. She shook her head while she made her point. And then the brim fell into her face and she stumbled off-balance like somebody who's drunk. That Mrs. Helsunk made her wear it during her speech and how could she talk convincingly with it on?"

"Maybe Bustle didn't want to be made into a hat. She wasn't used to being around people," Dawn said, looking at the hearth. Her Uncle Alex talked about flurries that were ghosts and the spirits of animals but she had never before seen anything strange happen with a pelt. Sometimes he said things to convince people that he knew the right way to cut a hide or a pelt from the carcass.

"It's so, Dawn. Bustle left her feathers at the inlet. And I've been sentimental about that swan," her father said, flapping a bellows at the fire. "But that hat doesn't do anything on its own. I've been around swans all my life. Their feathers are springy. It just shows those women the folly of display and extravagance. There's occasions for such a hat, especially if it's damp the day of the occasion. But your mother had to pick at her food, wearing it while she was eating."

"Now she probably won't wear it at all." Dawn thought of the native story, how the hunter woke up with only two feathers and a feeling of sadness. No one could really have any more than two swan feathers now.

"I won't make Petra wear it unless she wants to. She might like wearing it to the General Store. I guess I owe her a present that won't upset her with so much attention. We need to remind Mr. Reynolds about poaching. People are always askin' about things he doesn't stock. And the sheriff hasn't gotten his notices from Anchorage yet."

TWENTY-ONE

Only an hour after lunch recess, Miss Banrath handed back grammar papers. She usually did that right before the older children were dismissed for the day so that they could study their mistakes at home. Today, her face was as flushed as the strawberry red of her correcting pencil. Her hair, the tawny brown of a summer rabbit, was incomprehensibly crimped at the front.

"Dawn, your handwriting improved over the summer," she said in the half-whisper she used when she wanted to know more about one of her students. Dawn would have told her about the swan quill that was a talisman to her. But Miss Banrath hastened to the next student and when she walked by the window, she looked outside. Then she went to her desk and told everyone how her nephew's letter to a cannery had gotten him a job in Alaska. Miss Banrath's letters to her family convinced him to come to Alaska on a ship that was arriving in the harbor from Washington State. She let class out early that autumn day.

Dawn loped through leaves that rippled like salmon in a mossy stream. When she got home, she smelled coffee brewing in the kitchen but there, she was amazed to see her mother wearing the swan bonnet. Petra was sitting at the hearth, sewing together two pieces of sealskin. She turned in alarm but the swan feathers only nodded and the hat didn't slip.

"Why are you wearing the swan bonnet inside?" Dawn inquired bluntly.

"It has a calming effect when people aren't staring at it," her mother answered. Her mood was even more dreamy and distracted than Miss Banrath's had been.

Then her mother removed the hat and went to the hall. Dawn heard the cupboard door shut. It wasn't so startling a thing for her mother to be wearing clothes at home that she didn't wear to town. She hardly ever wore her native shirt with the feathers and ivory pieces sewn in unless it was an occasion like her birthday. When she wore skin pants in the garden, Petra told Dawn about a tribe of women and children who lived on the coast after the Russians left. They couldn't go back to their tribe after living with a Russian man and they couldn't go to Russia. That was in *her* grandfather's time. The women took the fishing boats out and they raised their children on the coast. Sealskin pants were traditional for those women, her mother said. That was why she didn't mind dressing as a boy when she worked on the salmon boat.

Once Dawn was seated in front of the supper potatoes to peel them, she wasn't sure that her mother heard the reason why she was home early. So she said, "Miss Banrath said my handwriting is improved. Since I started using Bustle's swan plume, it did. Why do you think the hat makes you feel calm?"

"It didn't seem right to be thinking about townsfolk manners when I was wearing it," her mother replied. "A swan would be ruffled on a town street. But that's not its nature. Your father still has ideas about its being a decoy."

"He thinks you might wear it to the General Store."

"Mr. Reynolds sells swan plumes there as if he's the only one around who has them."

As her mother started the fire in the stove, Dawn thought about Miss Banrath showing excitement and how her crimped hair kept her from looking so solemn. She was going to say that but Reindog was whining in the hall. This turned into a croon that he usually saved for full moon nights. Or when someone like Uncle Alex was approaching with another dog.

"What's the malamute howling about?" her mother asked.

Dawn went to the hallway and found Reindog with his paws planted under the high cupboard. Its door was teetering at the hinge and the swan hat was just visible, like a crescent moon. Dawn nudged the dog out of the way and then, when she couldn't reach inside the cupboard, she brought a crate out from Uncle Alex's room. She stood on it and pushed the hat far into the cupboard onto a folded blanket.

~~~

The next afternoon, Reindog wasn't jostling at the door when Dawn came in from school. He was sitting with his head jarred up under the hall cupboard. Its door was hanging askew and the swan bonnet was at the front of the cupboard again.

The malamute didn't follow Dawn to the hearth room as he usually did. Her mother must have worn the swan hat again for its calming effect and then she must have gone into town.

While Reindog squealed eerily, Dawn got onto the crate again but she couldn't resist lifting the hat out of the cupboard and setting it on her own head. The feathers floated at her cheeks. Once the hat was tied, she felt as if she were in a swirl of spring-warm snow.

She stepped off the crate and walked into the room that was to become a parlor. A small mirror was on the back of the door. She stood near the clutter of nets and the cot that Uncle Alex slept on when he was in town. Though the mirror was hazy, Dawn's reflection in the cloud of swans down and feathers was like the start of something. Just as a shelf in the room, displaying carved ivory, was the beginning of a parlor.

Reindog's tail lashed the welcome he didn't give her when she came in. But he sat without jumping, his blue-white eyes seeming to have feathers in them.

"What do you want this hat for?" Dawn asked the dog. "You didn't swim after Sir Swan and Bustle. I don't want you chewing on this hat."

Reindog had been taught not to chase the chickens in the yard but of course, her father wouldn't take him to swan migrations. They didn't take him the week before school started when she and her father went out to the inlet. Still, Pinion and Minion and their cygnets didn't come near the shore. Dawn could only admire the swan family from afar, the four cygnets gliding around their parents like boats around larger sea craft.

Grandma Glenda had explained it. "They came onto the yard once when we were inside. But they've been shunning our shore. I suppose it's because Bustle didn't swim back from it." The cygnets looked about ready to fly, stretching out their wings and stirring the water.

Dawn took off the swan hat and held it lower, out of Reindog's reach, waiting for him to launch himself. But the dog held back though he kept his frosty eyes on the hat. He sniffed and began to come closer to it. This time, Dawn stacked a muffler in front of the swan bonnet before shutting the cupboard door as well as she could.

In the kitchen, she rewarded the malamute with a piece of dried meat. Then she took out her tablet of paper and a sharpened pencil. He would actually pose for her, waiting for another reward. He looked stately as she drew him with the lines of a carving as if he were on a totem pole.

It made her think of the hat and the white birds that changed into people at night and then in the daytime, they flew away as birds again.

TWENTY-TWO

On Saturday, Dawn walked down the road to Clara Ann's house. They were going over to the Snow Clothing store because Clara Ann was impatient to see if Frances had finished a fur-trimmed hood for her.

At the store, Frances said, "It's fortunate that you got your order in early. We'll be knee-deep in orders when the weather changes."

Clara Ann tied on her hood and, after pondering herself in the wall mirror at Snow Clothing, was thrilled enough to immediately take it home to her mother. Frances also had a leather vest ready for her father.

"My father's coming home tonight," she told Dawn. "Now I can show my hood to him."

Clara Ann's father had been gone a month, working at the new railroad, and her mother, when they reached her door, had started on his homecoming dinner. Clara Ann had to help her.

Their house wasn't far from the ocean shore where only the local fishermen moored their boats. Near the harbor road, Dawn saw Oscar from school in a boat at the jetty near his house. This weekend, Oscar probably needed to know what happened at school because he was absent since Wednesday. He often missed school to help his brothers and his father with the day's fishing.

But on the hardened ground off the boardwalk, a strange man overtook Dawn.

"Miss, where are the nicest accommodations for a traveler with the money to pay for them?"

"Thaddeus's Hotel and Eatery. Up on the boardwalk," Dawn said.

"There ain't any better place? I'd like to spend the night in a nicer establishment. I couldn't get any sleep there."

Dawn kept walking but he caught up with her and said, "Might I buy you some refreshment there? I'm new to these parts."

He was at least Uncle Alex's age and seemed better fixed than most, wearing a well-sewed wool jacket and a felt hat. Dawn made for Oscar who seemed to be cleaning his boat.

"I guess you're native, sweetheart. The way those feathers are sewed on your hat. I could buy you a right good meal."

Dawn shook her head, continuing to walk, but the man pulled one of her braids. Mercifully, he let go so that she could run down to Oscar's boat.

She was on the jetty when Oscar saw the man walking onto it too. Oscar told her, "He's a bad one. He was shoutin' at that coast craft over there about someone owing him money."

Acting as if he hadn't seen Oscar, the man walked past Dawn on the jetty and then turned around towards her.

"Jump in the boat." Oscar untied it from the pier pole, and helped her down into his boat. Then they pushed off from the jetty.

"That little fox has eaten a meal with me before. She owes me something!" The man's sneer made his whiskers crooked over his teeth.

"He's lying," Dawn said to Oscar.

Oscar began steering his boat while he stared the man down. They floated off from him until they were watching his back.

"He's so bad he'd probably say that about Miss Banrath," Oscar said.

They could see him striding towards another fishing boat that was coming in.

"Lookin' for liquor," Oscar said. "They dock over near our boats sometimes when they're bringing it in. You want to sail near the smokehouse or ride in the boat a spell? I told my pa I'd throw out a net after I cleaned the boat."

"Let's sail a little," Dawn said. "I was over at Clara Ann's but she's got chores." Dawn hadn't known how short their afternoon would be. She expected that Clara Ann might want to visit the General Store or that they might walk by the church and the Helsunk's because it wasn't raining.

Though Dawn hadn't been on a boat with Oscar before, he was known to be as skilled with a fishing boat as his brothers. Sometimes he skipped whole weeks of school during the salmon runs in the spring.

Dawn's father knew Oscar's father well enough and while he would think it was fine if she walked on the boardwalk with Oscar, being in a boat with him was probably the safer thing. Oscar's brothers spent some evenings at Toddy's and Oscar resembled them.

"They bargain about the liquor right from the boats," he was saying. "They can toss it overboard if they see the deputy coming. And say it floated all the way from British Columbia."

It was true. Liquor was often hidden in the fishing nets as Mrs. Helsunk had said. Especially when sailors were about. It was said that fishing boats met larger craft offshore to get the liquor.

"Mrs. Helsunk has a mind to stop that," Dawn said.

"Her temperance society? I guess my mother didn't attend."

Oscar's mother had sewn up some of the nicest dresses Dawn had ever seen at church. Davy Shamison said that some could humble her because she once brought beer to men at a saloon up in Sitka when they still served it. Oscar's father had signed up as a sailor on a ship and when he came back, he brought her out of the saloon and stayed. Toddy knew her from before she was married and women like Mrs. Helsunk avoided talking to her after church.

"Have you ever gone anywhere on a ship, Oscar?"

"Went to Juneau once."

Dawn took off her straw hat since the breeze was buffeting it. She loved to look at the town from the water, nestled as it was under the masts of spruce. The clouds in the sky were unburdened and the air had sprays of sunshine in it.

Oscar was saying, "I want to join a ship, maybe next spring after the salmon run. I want to see the western coast. I don't s'pose I'd like the work they'd give me."

Still, Oscar had a pleased look on his face, the expression he usually wore at school. Because he didn't go every day, he seemed to enjoy it even if he wouldn't swallow some subjects as if they were forbidden bottles. Sometimes he did better at geography than anyone. He was like an otter, pleased to be on land, his hair shorn and browned up with a streak of sun. His blue eyes weren't like Captain Helsunk's; they were mild as the sky today.

They passed the houses that dotted the shore, nearing the arm of land that gave passage to the inlet where Dawn's grandparents lived. The forest line was so thick that the inlet wasn't visible until a boat was angled in its direction.

"I guess if I got on a whaling boat, I might have more to do," Oscar said. "Better than a ship that's just bringin' goods."

"Have you ever gone whaling?" Dawn said. "My uncle's been."

Oscar might appear scrawny to some of the men who went whaling.

"We were almost whaling in my father's boat once," Oscar said. "We were all ready with oars and spears and a gun. An angry calf near capsized our boat. We could see it thrashing right near the keel before it figured we weren't trying to keep it from its pod."

This was the only story of Oscar's that could impress Davy Shamison at school even if Oscar could read the clouds better. According to Davy, it was usual for Oscar to sit on a bench, staring into the air around Miss Banrath, and then look alert when she asked him a question. She thought he was better behaved than Davy. Davy couldn't think much of sitting out on the water, watching the spiral of gulls, and listening for the wind.

"It's calmer in the inlet," Dawn said. "You could throw your net out there." For all her mother knew, she might be practicing cable stitches with Frances. "Maybe we'll see my grandfather." Sometimes she went out in her grandfather's skiff if he came into town for a visit.

"Fishing's good at the mouth there," Oscar agreed. "The weather's not up though. I think that's him, over there."

Dawn saw some sails on the other side of the peninsula. The fishermen often took refuge from bad weather at the neck of the inlet.

"Past those boulders, we pulled up a nice net about a week ago," Oscar said.

Perhaps Miss Banrath couldn't put a cloud over Oscar because his father was known to chastise his boys. And he did that on days when they were already glum from struggling with the rain instead of a net full of fish.

"If we go in farther, we might see the swans." Dawn hadn't been near Pinion and Minion since July.

"It'd add some time. I guess I could say I looked for the sheriff after that bad one came out on the jetty."

"The deputy thinks a man like that is catch to haul in."

They had sailed past the boulders and into the middle of the inlet. Since the wind was brisk enough, Oscar kept the boat headed for the bay.

"You want to go on in to your grandparents?" he asked.

"No. I'd have to tell my grandma about that man. The swans have been staying on the far side of the bay. They might be around the shore where the bay opens."

Pinion and Minion nested on the north side of the bay where the foothills were below steep ridges. Since Dawn had missed the spring migration, all she had seen of the swans were Bustle and glimpses of the young resident family. It was like the native story about the two feathers, only the feathers were Bustle's hat. But the swans weren't usually so standoffish with boats. Sometimes they followed her grandfather as he sailed in.

"I'm not going to chase any swans," Oscar said. "I'll throw out my net and say I heard of a good catch over here."

He had seen the swans, turning where the inlet broadened. They were floating where Dawn last watched them, the four cygnets in a chasing mood, ruffling up when one was caught. Her grandfather's cabin was small on the far shore. Glenda liked the little fishing boats coming into the bay, relieving her isolation. Grandpa Fen tied red flannel to a sailboat mast or on the window if they wanted the fishermen to dock.

"You can get nearer, Oscar."

"You're losin' your hat," Oscar shouted.

She had forgotten to hold onto it. The straw hat was tumbling on her seat and filling with wind, about to become airborne. She leaned towards it, seeing the little feathers from Bustle flutter. Remembering how many more were in her pelt, she watched the wind take the straw hat to the water.

The straw hat bobbed on the waves while Oscar dropped his net and began to steer the craft towards the hat. It floated closer to the swans and they became distracted by it.

Oscar could maneuver the boat until he reached the hat with a net hook. But as he towed it in, the swans skidded away.

"There's some bread in the pail there," he said.

Pinion and Minion knew they could sometimes get feed from the fishermen. There were wheat buns in the pail. Dawn broke off large chunks, tossed a few, and then handed what was left to Oscar. He could toss them farther than she could.

It was a fine sight, the cygnets circling their parents as they swam towards the floating hunks of bread. They all needed to eat as much as they could with the migration coming. Dawn hoped that they were going on shore for the sunflowers and vegetables in Glenda's garden.

As the cygnets fought over the bread, they showed their burgeoning wings. Probably it was Pinion who nipped at them, keeping them at a distance from the boat.

TWENTY-THREE

When Dawn came back, it was so close to supper that her mother had done Dawn's part of it.

"Were you at Clara Ann's all day?" she demanded.

This would have been as unusual as being in Oscar's boat all afternoon.

"No, I was out in Oscar Forstad's boat."

"You were in a fishing boat all afternoon?" Her mother turned from the skillet of salmon that she was careful not to brown.

Dawn told her about the man in the wool jacket and how she and Oscar got away from him in his boat.

"Did he have a gun?"

"He might have."

"You're not to go down to the harbor by yourself."

"I wasn't at the harbor. Oscar was cleaning his boat out at the jetty near his house."

Young Fen was at the door, letting Reindog in. Petra went with a tin plate of stew bone for the dog and then Dawn heard her say, "Dawn was out in Oscar Forstad's boat. She says they took it from the jetty because a man followed her."

The dinner was a glum one during which Dawn was told that she had to ask permission to go out in a boat with any of the young fishermen. The subject had never come up before and it was on the tip of Dawn's tongue to remind her parents that her mother went on fishing boats. And that Oscar, a boy in school, was the least likely of any fishermen to be untrustworthy. But she knew that was the point, that if his older brother took her out in a boat, it might mean something else.

Her father said, "Boys like that can join up as sailors. Oscar's father did."

Her parents didn't regard the story about Oscar's father and mother the way they regarded their own. Most people thought it a lucky thing that Oscar's father wasn't as jealous as a miner who, thought dead, found his fiancé working in a Seward hotel and killed her. Stories like that even scared Frances, who said that if Paul came back, it would be better for her to be married than to have any reputation.

Petra said, "Now that school's started, you've got things to do at home too. You can't accompany Clara Ann on the boardwalk and take all afternoon."

Young Fen added, "I could use some help with that fence I'm fixin'."

Dawn couldn't argue but when Reindog began whining, she said, "Uncle Alex should be coming any day now." He usually came back from the north when the ships were in port for their last trips before the winter.

"Have you gotten word on buying the gully land?" Petra asked.

"No, it takes time with the paperwork," Young Fen said.

Even though this was a sore point since their horses and cow might drink from the gully after the spring melt, Dawn was glad the subject had changed.

Petra asked, "What's the use of moving the log fence to the other side of the gully if they decide the property isn't yours?"

"I want it built before the spring. The boundary line is the gully. And no one wants to build on the hill behind it."

"What's the use of a boundary line when you can get around it with a log fence?" Petra's fork clattered to the table when Reindog made a persistent low howl. If it was the swan bonnet causing him to do this, Petra might take it upstairs this time. Dawn wanted to try it on once more.

"To think how I trembled taking wages when I dressed as a boy," Petra was saying. "I shuddered at what they'd do if they found out on the fishing boat. You men are like the tides of the ocean about the rules you set. If you've made a boundary or a rule, you should stick to it."

"That's just the trouble!" Dawn's father said. "The men who set the boundary don't know this piece of land. It's nothin' to them to set it ten feet farther. Half of the gully is mine for sure. Why should my fence keep it from the thirsty animals? When the water's coming down, the stream brings in the wild animals."

Dawn put in, "Nobody wants land unless the rocks in it are gold. What if we found a piece of gold in the gully? Washed down in the spring?"

Her mother replied, "If that happened, we'd have to fight in court over our own land. Just as if Alex had gotten himself a bear and the wolves were waiting on the tundra."

Young Fen was chewing a pout while a howl in the hallway made the sound of frustration. The wind had begun swishing like reeds as the dog crooned. "What's that dog howling about? Someone might be outside, speaking of Alex."

"I'll go look," Dawn offered.

In the hall, Reindog sat under the high cupboard as if he were at loggerheads with it. The cupboard door was ajar again and when she looked inside, Dawn saw swan feathers. It reminded Dawn that the migration was imminent and that even though they were left with Bustle's hat, the swans might want to take that back too if they knew. She hadn't minded letting her straw hat go.

Dawn drove the malamute off with the crate from Uncle Alex's room but when she stood on it, she found the hat leaning from the muffler she set there. She shook the bent feathers and set the hat behind the muffler again, thinking that her mother had worn it while she was in Oscar's boat. But it must have been thrown in the cupboard, perhaps because her mother heard her at the door and hurried.

Returned to the supper table, Dawn had to say, "Reindog was howling at the swan bonnet."

"I'll store that hat upstairs," Petra said. "I wore it the other day to be at peace with it. But it's like wearing a law on my head outside. I haven't put it on since."

This puzzled Dawn, especially because *she* had put it on since. "The cupboard door is loose on its hinges."

"I'll get to that," her father said. "See, even Reindog is inquiring about the hat. I was sayin', we'll go into the General Store when the migration begins and have a sit on the verandah there. Sheriff Farefax says he's got to have the notices printed the way they are in the States and he can't do them in town. Every time I ask him about it, he says they're on the way. Instead of people talking about the location of the swans, I want them talking about what'll happen if they're caught with a pelt."

"They'll be accusing if I'm wearing the swan bonnet," Petra sighed.

Ready to sit on the verandah too, Dawn said, "The last swan hat in Alaska, made from a priceless pelt."

"Now here we're talking about swans again," her father said, pushing his plate back and getting up for a toothpick. "You'll have to be careful talking on the subject. Don't tell about your grandparents or the trail to the inlet when you're at school, Dawn. You hear?"

"What if poachers follow Grandpa Fen's boat?"

"Then they're on foot or in a boat. Pretty easy to catch that way."

"Someone needs to be on the lookout."

"Someone will be."

Dawn persisted, "Then someone should be near the road and someone else on the north side. Can't I go out and help Grandma Glenda? Miss Banrath took an afternoon off when her nephew shipped up here."

"Migrating swans aren't your relatives. If you miss school, it'll get around," her father said.

Even if her parents kept her inside now, Dawn was glad that she had seen Pinion and Minion and their cygnets up close, probably for the last time this year. She decided not to argue if her mother stored the hat away. How the swan hat migrated to the front of the cupboard, looking as if it wanted to waft away, was disturbing. She couldn't imagine her mother putting it back in such a precarious way. With the cupboard door coming open and Reindog baying as if he were waiting for something, the hat might never be worn on her mother's head again or on hers.

TWENTY-FOUR

Petra didn't store the hat away that night. In the morning, Dawn was the first to get up for a gusty and gloomy day. Her mother left with her father after breakfast, wearing her hare hat to Frances's. The last in the house, Dawn was wrapping her books in a hide bag when she saw that the hall cupboard door was askew on its hinge again.

Thinking that the wind burst in when her parents left, she dragged the crate to the cupboard and said to Reindog, planted now at the parlor door, "At least you're not whining under the cupboard. Where the swan hat is. Swan hat!"

Dawn thought she might be dreaming and the swan hat had taken wing and migrated right out the door. She had watched her mother to see if she would store it upstairs. Maybe her father put it somewhere. Or her mother might have taken the hat to Frances's. That was it, she thought, closing the cupboard door. Her mother and Frances were going to alter the hat.

Dawn would have shaken the hood over her head and gone to school except that Reindog didn't follow her to the door as usual. Instead, he sat sniffing and whimpering at the parlor door. Though he was being trained to stay out of that room, he didn't usually mope about it. Dawn looked into the room, expecting to find her Uncle Alex sleeping on the cot in his clothes. But there was a law of Uncle Alex's nature and that was to have the parlor door closed when he visited. The empty cot, flush against the wall, had fishing nets, dog harnesses, and blankets on it. Then Dawn glimpsed something white under the cot, not a pillow with a feather escaping, but the swan bonnet.

She fished up the hat, shook the dust off it, and put it into the cupboard, in the back again. Then she secured the door and waited to

---

make sure that it didn't totter from the hinge. Doubting that there would be a swan memento when she was grown up, Dawn considered the distance that the hat covered, wondering how it traveled across the parlor floor and concealed itself under the cot.

She slid into the schoolroom late, still puzzled and worried that the dog had gotten hold of the hat and couldn't help but show what he had fetched. According to the native story, a pelt could vanish as swiftly as a swan. And then, Miss Banrath read a poem called "The Wild Swans of Coole." It was from a book her nephew gave her by an Irishman named Yeats.

Dawn felt as if she had feathers on her spine as Miss Banrath read:

> *The trees are in their autumn beauty*
>
> *The woodland paths are dry,*
>
> *Under the October twilight the water*
>
> *Mirrors a still sky:*
>
> *Upon the brimming water among the stones*
>
> *Are nine-and-fifty swans.*

Here she had to be quiet about swans when the poem made her think of the last migration she saw at the inlet, a year ago. At the end, Miss Banrath read in a melancholy tone:

> *when I awake someday*
>
> *To find they have flown away?*

Mystified about swans and spirits, Dawn found Clara Ann at morning recess. She told her friend about the bewildering hat so that she wouldn't talk about migrations, expecting a splash of sense. A full minute passed while Clara Ann mulled over this and then she said, "That's easy. The muffler fell down and the dog grabbed the end of it. He's big enough to jump that high. Then the swan bonnet got pulled down and he hid it."

"But the muffler was still in the cupboard," Dawn said. "And the hat didn't look like it had any teeth marks on it. I think Reindog was trying to tell me it was there."

"Someone took it down from the cupboard then. Your dog got hold of it and hid it like a bone." Clara Ann admitted that the swan hat was special but not so special as to be supernatural. Two other girls clustered to the conversation, listening at the word *swan*.

Dawn suddenly wondered if sled dogs could outrun Captain Helsunk's motorcar. Clara Ann mused on this and Agnes Reynolds said she would ask her father about a race. When Agnes began talking grandly about motorcars and the subject of swans was forgotten, Dawn thought about the swan bonnet again. Miss Banrath with her nine-and-fifty wild swans made her feel that there was superstition at school too.

As Davy Shamison strutted by, Dawn decided to tell him about the swan bonnet during the afternoon recess. Oscar wasn't in school. His brother had been waiting for him when he brought her back in their boat.

Davy scorned the idea that the swan hat had the gumption to glide through doors. He didn't believe that Reindog would only sniff at it. But the malamute did know enough to take a pelt to the cot where Alex Tuskoffey slept.

"Somebody was careless with it," Davy summed up. "It's not flyin' around in the night and hiding under beds. Sounds as if you're thinking a hat is like you, sailing from that man down at the harbor. Well, we went after him. He was playing cards for liquor."

"Your father got him?"

"Yup. There's a man at Toddy's who's delivering liquor by boat. He gets it in Canada. Just started his business here. The one that followed you is on his way to Anchorage."

Dawn told Davy about the swan bonnet in the awesome way that her Uncle Alex told about the ghosts of winter. If she said that the swan bonnet was a decoy, he would probably deride her father for it. But Davy didn't seem to think that there was any swan spirit about it even if he believed that animals could smell a fight in a man and could cause fighting between hunting men.

"It sounds like you've got some sort of native idea in your head, Dawn," Davy said. "I guess you know what they'd think of it, being kin. That the swan spirit is angry about the way it died."

"It died of old age," Dawn said, even though she worried that Bustle wouldn't like being made into a hat.

"It did!" Davy snorted as if he'd been along at her grandparents'. "I'm going to ask Kenny about it. He knows about that stuff. More than Mrs. Helsunk knows about things being possessed."

"But you don't understand how the swan died. You've never even been to the inlet as far as I know."

"Course I have," Davy said nonchalantly. "I suppose you wouldn't know if your Grandpa Fen ever took a glass."

"A glass of what?" Dawn asked.

"Whiskey, cloudberry wine, vodka," Davy cocked his head. "It's for the good of all that my pa's been chasing down the spirits of alcoholic drink since I can remember. That's a possession that makes souls act different and mostly derelict. Why, that man at the harbor, he had a bottle that smelled of liquor in his room. We stopped by your grandfather's like anyone else's. All those berries your grandmother gathers, she could be making wine. But you folks always want to talk about swans, maybe to change the subject."

Replying, Dawn stressed, "If you'd seen that swan this summer, you'd know it could hardly swim anymore. And that there aren't as many swans as there used to be. Sheriff Farefax knows that it's not just here, either. He's got to put up notices again. As soon as they come in."

"Like when Sheriff Farefax officially closed the bars. It's my pa had to keep them closed and ride the country chasing ninety-proof spirits. Sheriff Farefax, he's got to keep his eye on the harbor and on any fighting that happens over at Toddy's. I might be ridin' out with my pa to keep an eye out for poachers. Have the swans started migrating yet?"

"But you come to school every day. When could you ride out with your father?" Dawn pointed out. "The migrators will probably come during the school week." Thinking about fathers, she realized she had gotten on the subject of migrating swans. Anyway, Mrs. Shamison probably wasn't allowing Davy to bust stills after school. He came almost every day with his homework done.

Davy grinned and his granite eyes flashed disarmingly. "Weekends and summer days I ride out plenty. Sometimes after school. That colt we got last spring is mine now. I broke her in."

"You ride it in your back pasture," Dawn said, still not persuaded that Davy went along on Deputy Shamison's chases. She recalled an evening after her father bought Bustle's pelt. Uncle Alex told the price of the colt that Deputy Shamison obtained from a breeder in Anchorage. Then as he warmed his hands at the hearth, he said that Deputy Shamison paid as much as some people paid for a swan pelt. "You mean you've got that colt trained to ride in the foothills?"

"Already," Davy said. "But how could you see me leaving our back pasture? That's how nobody expects the deputy."

Davy tilted his face towards the spruce-feathered mountains. Dawn could imagine him riding off as suddenly as an eagle annoyed into flight. She thought it would be thrilling to gallop on a lithe horse and see a swan migration. Her mother's horse, Lead-Boy, was a wagon horse and would carry her grudgingly. In a few afternoon hours, a horse like Davy's would glide to the inlet, take its water while its rider watched swans, and soar home for supper.

Davy might have trailed her thoughts. He looked guardedly at the other boys, boys that he probably wished to be along with just then.

"I think I saw a swan flying this morning, early," he said. "Maybe the migration is starting. I bet you just don't know that, just like you never can tell when your Uncle Alex is goin' to stay at your house."

It was true. They couldn't tell when Grandpa Fen would see a cloud of swans outside his window.

Davy continued, "Folks that stay up late at night might have seen them. I could have seen one that fell behind."

Dawn took heed of Davy's jutting nose and sharp eyes, glinting like feldspar now. Her father probably didn't mean to keep the deputy from knowing about the migration. Deputy Shamison said he'd help with it if he could.

"They're not migrating yet. That must have been a goose you saw." It wouldn't hurt to have Davy on lookout though. "I hope they don't migrate during the school week. Then I can't go and watch them."

"I guess I'd like to see a migration so much that I'd skip school for it. Miss Banrath would understand about wild swans if she found out. I'd jump on my horse the minute I heard about a migration."

As Dawn began brooding about this, Davy leapt off to a group of boys who were shooting rocks at a target drawn with chalk on a tree.

~~~

The next morning, Dawn took her schoolbooks to the hall, imagining a day when she might skip school. But then she saw the swan hat hanging on the coat rack. The cupboard door flapped open above it.

Pondering this, she asked her mother in the kitchen, "Are you going to wear the swan hat today?"

"Why should I?" her mother wondered.

"I don't know. Because it makes you feel calm." Dawn paused at her coffee cup as if it perplexed her. Then she saw that her father was watching her mother instead of eating his fried egg.

"Not when I'm walking on the boardwalk," her mother said.

Then Reindog barked to be let in the back door. After he came in and cantered to the hall, he started whining. In the hallway, Dawn found him on his haunches, his tail waving like a great plume. She unhooked the swan hat from the coat rack and put it up in the cupboard. Then she found the crate, got up on it, and tidied the muffler in front of the hat.

In the kitchen, Dawn announced, "I just put the swan hat back in the cupboard. It was on the coat rack. Do you think the wind blew in and the cupboard came open and the swan hat floated to the rack?"

She didn't say the last part with much conviction. Still, her parents might accuse her of playing with the hat.

Her father squinted at her mother, his mutton chops making a shrug. "I didn't take it out of the cupboard."

Petra had a plate of flapjacks in her hands. It fell on the table and the flapjacks made a landslide.

"I don't know how it got there," she said, but her voice was as wan as her face.

"It's spooky," Dawn said. She didn't say how many times the hat had strayed from the cupboard though. And for all she knew, the migrating swans might have come today.

Dawn's father stepped into the hallway. When he came back, he was wearing his hide jacket, ready to depart. "That hat floating is as spooky as your Uncle Alex and his swan people," he said. "I'll ask if he's in town, Petra. He probably stopped by too late and left the hat out as a practical joke. He wasn't happy to lose that swanskin to me."

~~~

At school, Dawn sat in the room adjoining the main room, writing out answers concerning crops and livestock in the States. Oscar was laboring in the next chair and even though she pointed out to him that he'd spelled the word *wheat* as *wheet*, when he elevated his blue eyes, his expression became pleased. Davy was watching as Oscar corrected his tablet, his granite eyes gleaming, and then he rolled them towards the main room.

Miss Banrath was watching young Kenny as he carved at his pencil with a pocket knife. Someone in the back was reading about three farm children and two pond ducks. Kenny had been caught before, carving his pencil or a piece of wood in class. Then he had to read aloud about the children stationed around the ducks and how they tried to make them come to shore with cake and bread and turnip greens.

Even as Dawn spelled out the state name *Missouri* and turned her paper so that Davy could see it since his mother came from there, she kept thinking about swans and the time her Uncle Alex brought an eider duck that he shot. Before it was plucked for its feathers and roasted, he hung it on the hall rack.

Uncle Alex never displaced their things though. He left furs, a knapsack, a heap of sled blankets, a goose, or a duck. His ghosts were polar bears, silver wolves, and hoary foxes, seen in a purple twilight. And the bird people who acted like ghosts. Still, Uncle Alex would not have come two nights in a row, once to slide the swan hat under his cot and the second time to hang it on the coat rack.

Dawn thought about the swan plume at home, how it anchored her hand when she was drawing. Then she imagined the swan hat wafting like a leaf from a tree and landing on the coat rack.

Her mother wanted to be at peace with the hat. It fell off of her head, it tickled her nose when she was talking, and if it crimped, its feathers flared.

People in their town expected the mishap instead of anything falling into place. Men talked of storms as if they were mistakes; sailors prepared for welcome mats of ice; miners readied for anything when they used dynamite. To people like her, a hat resting so politely on a coat rack of its own accord was downright chilling. It would be as if the pond ducks put the cake and bread thrown to them on lily pads before eating it.

~~~

At recess, Oscar and the other boys were playing with some new clay marbles that came into Reynolds's store. Clara Ann was sitting on a bench nearby but before Dawn reached her, Davy jumped up from the marbles game and walked alongside, turning towards the harbor.

"I think I saw a few swans flyin' last night," he said.

"Are you sure?" Dawn did her homework now at her window upstairs, watching after sundown. She decided to mystify Davy with the swan hat appearing on the coat rack. "Neither of my parents could account for it. My father thought that my Uncle Alex might have stopped by. They probably think I put it there but I didn't."

"I don't think your Uncle Alex is in town. My pa mentions it if he is," Davy replied.

"The hinge is loose on the cupboard but I'd expect the hat would float to the floor if it fell out."

"Maybe there's something to that spirit stuff. Maybe the swans are migrating." Davy looked out at the harbor, his eyes fixed, as if he were watching someone. Sometimes Dawn didn't know whether to distrust him or to like him.

Then his eyes caught the light and he was sprightly. "I'd ride out on my colt to see if the swans are here. You could ride on the other horse. Lottie'd be just right for you."

"I might know tomorrow. When could we ride out?" Dawn blurted. She knew that if her grandmother didn't come to town today or if her grandfather sailed in just to talk to her father, the swans were migrating.

Davy's face kept its edges as he said secretly, "Right after school. We could go to our pasture and ride out from there. It doesn't take so much time as sailing to the inlet. We could even go after lunch. We'll tell Miss Banrath that we're goin' out with my pa to watch for poachers."

Although Dawn's father talked of being a vigilante, he was against her helping. Yet she couldn't imagine her father ever skipping a swan migration because he had to go to school. He didn't usually miss migrations except last spring and that was because the swans were scared off.

"Miss Banrath might keep a secret about the swans. But I'm not supposed to tell anyone about the migration," Dawn said, adding, "She hardly ever talks to my mother. We could say we're helping to post notices. I guess they came in. Just in time too. If my grandmother doesn't come into town today, maybe you saw swans."

They were coming any day if they were coming, and Davy probably knew the back roads to the inlet.

"Look, there's Kenny. Let's tell him about the hat." Davy steered Dawn from Oscar who had shot a marble near them.

Kenny sat under a spruce, carving at a chunk of wood. He listened to the unaccountable landings of the swan bonnet with the quiet that his father had at the salmon smokehouse. His eyebrows stayed level but his eyes gleamed like a caribou calf's.

"What do you think, Kenny?" Davy demanded. "Do you think the swan spirit was angry about the way it died?"

Dawn protested, "The old swan couldn't get around anymore. She probably couldn't have flown at migration time."

"But so many swans have been killed without respect," Kenny said. "My father says people kill them for the money that gives respect. But since swans don't kill, it's no honor to kill them like grizzlies."

"My grandparents treated the old swan well," Dawn said. "They fed it sunflower seeds and corn. There was poaching last spring before Bustle died. My grandparents didn't see her mate. Maybe someone poached him."

"I don't know if a swan would want to be made into a hat like that," Kenny said, looking at her sidelong. "Usually, women sew the feathers into their clothing."

Davy walked off as Dawn told Kenny about the mishaps her mother had with the hat. Then she told him about the old swan's swansong. Over her voice, Davy and some other boys were making noises like motorcar exhaust.

TWENTY-FIVE

Saying she had homework to do, Dawn left the supper table that evening and went upstairs instead of sitting by the hearth. She sat in kerosene light through the entire twilight, gazing out of her window at the cloud frost on the mountain. Grandma Glenda hadn't come in to market, her father said.

Because the salmon and halibut had to be smoked for the fall ships, Dawn's father stayed in town until he was sure that the swans had come. But this year, Grandpa Fen wasn't fishing in case of poachers. Dawn watched the moon hide behind clouds dark as sealskin, realizing that she and Davy would have to conceal themselves in the brush. She tried to decide whether she should tell Miss Banrath the truth about the migration or whether she should lie about the notices. She could get found out either way. Miss Banrath, being enthralled with the nine-and-fifty swans, might talk with her father sometime.

On this, Dawn fell asleep. The next thing she knew though, she was awake, sloped in her bed so that the mountain was in her view. It was past midnight, the moon having journeyed across the sky. Except for a creaking downstairs in the hearth room, the house was silent. The creaking was probably Reindog, Dawn thought, restless under a full moon.

She took her pillow to her bedroom chair where she gazed at the moonlight that gave the mountain the deepest blue of an Alaskan lupine. Then she saw snowy flickers off from the precipices. They floated down like huge petals. Swans!

For minutes, Dawn watched the circling swans. They probably went as far as the ocean and then turned around to the inlet. The night was almost windless; it would be clear brisk autumn at daybreak. Being so awake, she decided to get herself a glass of milk and look out from the back door. The creaking had stopped; the dog was probably curled on the hearthrug, snoozing noisily.

As Dawn counted the number of stairs in the dark, she heard a voice at the stairwell, probably someone speaking to Reindog. On the last step, she expected to see her Uncle Alex admiring pelts in the dim firelight. Or her father might have seen the swans. She would probably have to go back upstairs at once.

When she looked into the hearth room though, she saw her mother shawled in a blanket, sitting near the dark hearth, and wearing the swan hat.

"Mother!" Dawn called softly, thinking that the swan hat was so calming that it helped her mother sleep.

"There's no use pushing through the drifts, Alex." Her mother's voice was eerie.

"Ma," Dawn said more loudly, going into the hearth room. Her mother must be sleep talking.

"They're buried in that coffin of snow. Remember what she said about heaven? They dress like swans there."

"It's me, Dawn!" Dawn was afraid to shake her mother awake. Her father said that when she was sleepwalking, she sometimes threw herself at a wall as if it were a block of ice. She hadn't been sleepwalking for years.

Her mother mumbled, "The land has had its revenge. He's clamped in a snare of ice."

Dawn ran upstairs and woke her father. Because he had spent nights on a salmon boat, his slumber was as steady as a boat on the waves. By the time he got downstairs, Petra had gone to the hall. Then they saw her in Uncle Alex's room, putting the swan hat on the cot there.

"Petra! You're sleepwalking!" Dawn's father yelled.

"I know," she murmured. "The bobsled is buried in the snow too." But she shook her head and began to be alert.

Young Fen took her by the arm and led her into the kitchen. He lit the lamp and pulled a drawer all the way out of the kitchen cabinet. From its cavity, he withdrew a bottle like the rubbing lineament that Uncle Alex kept for his chapped skin.

"Drink the brandy," he said to Petra.

Dawn didn't know if she had ever smelled brandy before but this was the same smell as the lineament bottle.

"I had that dream again," Petra said. "The snow was turning into shining garments."

"Go on up to bed, Dawn," her father commanded. "And don't tell anyone about the brandy bottle. It's for medicinal purposes. Even Captain Helsunk kept one bottle of brandy on his ship for calming people after storms. He won't talk about that now."

There were swans again, flying in a small luminous vector across the foothills. Dawn admired them until she heard the door to her parents' room shut. She counted swan wings until she could sleep.

~~~

In the morning, Young Fen said that it might do Petra good to see the migration.

But the dream picture of snow and swan coverings in the sky was ominous to her. The migrating swans seemed to be in front of her eyes.

"I'll get the horses ready," she said. "I guess Glenda shouldn't be patrolling alone if poachers are about."

"I don't mean today," he said. "I s'pose you're not in any mood to wear the swan bonnet today, are you?"

"I'd feel as if I was sleepwalking," she said.

"I'd like ta stop poachers from going out there instead of encountering them at the inlet. The swans should still be there in a few days. You might go out there, maybe Dawn too, if it seems alright. Why, folks might have seen them from Toddy's last night. They weren't any dream, flying towards the inlet."

It was the day when the swan bonnet might work as a decoy if Petra could force herself to put it on. But the notices had gone up and that should remind folks. A ship was in port with sailors and travelers who wouldn't understand the swan bonnet. Hunters were another thing. They knew that if the swan was made into a hat, its pelt wasn't being sold as smuggled export.

Young Fen left early, to have breakfast at Toddy's and to see if anyone was talking about swans. When Dawn came down, Petra felt abashed. Dawn hadn't seen her sleepwalking before. Petra sat in front of the hearth fire, toasting bread, and said, "I guess the swan hat started up my old sleepwalking dreams. You'd think it had a spirit to do that."

She was puzzled to have dreamed of swans on the very night when they were migrating.

Dawn replied, "The other day, I found the swan bonnet under the cot in Uncle Alex's room. Do you think you were sleepwalking then?"

This frightened Petra. She thought that Young Fen always noticed her sleepwalking.

"I got to talking with Davy Shamison and we asked Kenny about swan spirits. He didn't think Bustle would want her pelt made into a hat like that. But if you put it on when you were sleepwalking, the dream spirit in you wanted it on."

"I suppose Kenny would say that," Petra replied.

"He thinks it's fine that women wear the feathers in shirts."

"Course he would. Your father's in a fierce Irish spirit about those swans. But he said that if there's no trouble, we'll go out to the inlet to see them."

"I suppose he means Saturday." Dawn went to the hall and put on her hood. At the door, she said, "Davy invited me to come and see his colt after school."

Petra went after Dawn but she was running to school. Davy Shamison hadn't ever invited Dawn to see his colt before and to see a colt was to want a ride on a colt.

Petra kept seeing swan feathers in front of her. Because the swan hat was real, she might feel better wearing it. She didn't usually meet Dawn after school but she could go to the General Store in the afternoon and see the notice put up there. Then she might walk on down to the school. Dawn had gone sailing with Oscar and now she might ride Davy's colt. Petra was only a few years older than Dawn when she and Young Fen went up to Sitka to get married. But she didn't have any parents at home.

~~~

After Dawn hastened through the ragtag of fall, the morning lagged. She kept thinking of Grandma Glenda patrolling the inlet. If there was trouble, her grandmother's Irish spirit could be as fierce as her father's about the swans. She knew that if Davy was ready to ride, she couldn't resist even if they would have to hide from her father. Dense woods were behind the inlet trail. She figured they could cut down from the road and see the migration closer to the mouth of the inlet where the ground was high and they might see her father coming.

"I saw swans last night in the moonlight," she whispered to Davy while Miss Banrath taught the younger students. He shrugged but his nonchalance was probably to fool people.

On the schoolyard at recess, he almost walked by her though, his eyes like pebbles.

"Davy, are you going to ride out? The swans are migrating!"

"I already know." He grinned but it might have been at Oscar who was standing nearby.

"You could ask Miss Banrath about going to see wild swans. I could say my mother isn't feeling well and that there's things to do at home. It wouldn't be a lie. That way, it won't look as if we're riding out together. If we went at lunchtime, we'd be back late afternoon."

She would have told Davy about the hat causing her mother to sleepwalk but his eyes were on the ground. After last night, she wondered if Davy would ever see her mother wear it again. She wondered if she would see any more migrations if the swans kept getting scared up.

Davy was flicking rocks and pebbles with his foot as if they were clay marbles. "I can't take my horse anywhere. One of its horseshoes needs lookin' at cause he's growing. That's what Pa said and my ma, she'll tell him if the colt's gone."

Dawn would have hated Davy except that his smile turned apologetic, saucy as it was. The rest of the day was entirely uneventful and so trying that she wanted to tell Miss Banrath that her mother wasn't feeling well and she might go home. She had discussed the migration and might have been caught at the inlet if they had ridden there. She might even have told Davy about her mother's sleepwalking and then it wouldn't be just a hat that made her a laughingstock. Especially when the only event that day was her mother waiting outside the school and wearing the swan hat. Miss Banrath had to have a talk with her about it.

TWENTY-SIX

Dawn didn't see her father to ask about the swans. He was riding out to the inlet and when he wasn't there, he was at the smokehouse. She and her mother had walked near the harbor after school because her mother heard at the General Store that Uncle Alex was in town.

Friday night, Dawn sat up watching for white wings in the shadow of the mountain. But she saw no more swans, only the moonlight wheeling around the peaks. In the morning, she awoke to hear metal clanging like a bell. Downstairs, her mother was holding an empty frying pan and pondering her egg basket and some bulbous potatoes.

"I guess I didn't notice we needed food from the store yesterday," she said, and then briskly, "Hurry up and put on your clothes. We'll eat breakfast at Thaddeus's if you're quick."

When Dawn went into the hall for her hide jacket, she found her mother tying on the swan hat at the mirror in Uncle Alex's room. Then she walked to the door as if she were sleepwalking. "Put your hat on. Maybe we'll discourage poachers from a clash with your father," she said.

"Do you think someone from here was out poaching at the inlet last spring?" Uncle Alex might be suspected when Dawn knew that he didn't hunt at the inlet during migrations.

"That's what your father wants to find out," Petra said as they walked out into the gray day. "But if it's any hunters come to town, we might divert them the way Alex does with his gold nugget. Why, even Miss Banrath was wondering about the migrating swans."

"She was wondering if people were watching for poachers. Uncle Alex keeps saying there are lots of swans up north, swans nobody sees to count," Dawn said as they took the dirt road to the boardwalk.

"I wonder if Frances has seen him. We'll ask her if she wants to eat breakfast at Thaddeus's," Petra replied. The day spilt around them in puddles that were overcast like the clouds. At the boardwalk, people were out already and they stared at the hat. Dawn and her mother skirted them slowly enough for them to inquire but they were solemn as the puddles. At Snow Clothing, Petra put a parcel of fur boots on the counter.

"You're wearing the swan bonnet," Frances said. "And the notices were just put up. Whatever possessed you?"

Petra and Dawn stood before the postings on the wall. "I've got nothing to be ashamed of," Petra said. "But maybe I can find out who knows about the back roads." Then she spoke to Frances at the counter. "Have you seen Alex?"

"No. But some ship people asked if he'd come back from up north. About three days ago."

"It's about time Sheriff Farefax got those notices printed up," Petra said.

"They're as important as the Prohibition notices. But the old tankard said that they didn't come in when it was expected. It's too bad, people think they can get around him on Prohibition," Frances said.

"They think they can do anything in a territory town. And the notices going up now just remind people of the swans. Would you like to eat breakfast with us at Thaddeus's?"

"Sure I would. Someone should be with you when you wear that hat right now."

"I don't think a catalog hat will ever go over in this town," Petra remarked.

"You flatter me talking about catalogs. I'll wear my hat with the arctic hare fur."

"While you lock up, I've got some things to get at the General Store. We'll meet you at Thaddeus's." Turning to leave, Petra said to Dawn, "I think your father is going to take us to the migration tomorrow."

"We'll take the wagon?" Dawn said.

"He doesn't like to sail through the migrating swans. Frances, if you want to take in the sight, Dawn can sit in the wagon."

"My father went out to the inlet with Young Fen yesterday," Frances said. "He said it was a fine sight. Maybe Young Fen wants to ride on horseback. We might drive the wagon."

Dawn was thrilled and they would celebrate today at Thaddeus's. Her mother hadn't gone to a migration with them since Pinion and Minion stayed their first summer.

"As long as there's no trouble out there," Petra added.

~~~

It was difficult to translate the looks Petra received because of the sea mist from the harbor. But a man in a red and black logging jacket shouted out, "How'd you get that hat, Woman?"

"It's a family memento. The swan died a natural death," Petra said into the air. "The sheriff can tell you about this hat."

"They say those notices weren't up this time last year," the man said, so close that Dawn could see his beard bristling.

She answered, "There were notices up but they got ripped down."

"Swans are a scarce sight around here." Petra said, not so begrudging of conversation today. "You won't see another hat like this. It wasn't gotten illegally."

At the verandah of the General Store, a woman and a group of men watched them the way people watched Captain Helsunk's motorcar when he drove through town. As Petra walked towards the store door, the piqued men hung back, clearing the way so they could stare at the hat.

Inside, Dawn went to the counter where she could keep track of what her mother bought and pretend she was more interested in the peanut brittle. The stares were overbearing. She felt as if she were a pallbearer to a swan and that the men inside the store didn't care.

Mr. Reynolds came out from around the counter to help Petra.

"Good morning, Petra. Flour today?" His voice lowered. "I hear Glenda might be in with a parcel of plumes. I've been saying I'm plumb out of them."

Petra turned away from Mr. Reynolds, causing him to survey the men standing amongst the wares. "The fish mates are scorning me," she said.

A wry voice replied. "It's Petra that's tauntin' the town with that hat. I was just reading this posting over here. And it was our landlubbing salmon buyer who put it up. Remember, we used to call him Swan Boy?"

Near the two fishermen in rain hats were two men in hide jackets listening intently.

Petra stepped towards the fishermen. "If you're set on talking, you might mention that no one here can hunt swans. That includes Young Fen."

"I didn't think you were one to flaunt good fortune," the other fisherman said in a teasing way. "To think you were once a net mender and rigged up pretty oddly too. If you didn't sell the swan that's on your head, you must be doing pretty well."

"We didn't sell that swan pelt on principle, Sam. There aren't swan pelts here to sell except what dies naturally. Anyone who buys the plumes here knows that, don't they?" Petra said this squarely, having turned towards Mr. Reynolds.

Dawn watched four more men come into the store, one who stood near the notices on the wall and the other three standing near the tobacco tins.

Mr. Reynolds replied, "Swan Feathers. Collected from Live Swans. That's the note that's tacked to the empty barrel there." He pointed to a shelf behind the counter.

The first fisherman blustered, "I don't know, Petra. Alex used to say there was something wrong in your head. I still think that pertains, wearing that swan hat after these notices have gone up."

"It's interesting to see who gets drawn to swan feathers right now," Petra said to that. "And it's interesting to see who has the law in their mouth. You might as well taunt Deputy Shamison after he's confiscated some cloudberry wine."

Mr. Reynolds said near Dawn, "I wouldn't taunt the person whose been asking about feathers lately."

When Dawn asked who it was, he wondered if she wanted some peanut brittle.

Petra said, "We're going to have some flapjacks with maple syrup over at Thaddeus's."

They bought a few pieces of peanut brittle anyway and paid up. But as they were leaving, each with a burlap sack, the second fisherman called out, "Good to see you, Petra. You're sure looking a woman these days. Pardon my suspicions. I used to say..."

He might have said what he used to say but then he was noticing Dawn instead.

Her mother replied, "I've suspicions too. I don't know why this hat isn't talked of as the family memento that it is."

Dawn had gone ahead to the door and couldn't help but look towards the jeers when she was suddenly thrust towards her mother. Flour misted the air as Mrs. Helsunk burst in. Even Mrs. Helsunk couldn't muster words as Dawn regained her balance and her mother mumbled, "Excuse us, Mrs. Helsunk."

"Like I said the other day, Mrs. Helsunk. No swan feathers this week," Mr. Reynolds called out.

TWENTY-SEVEN

That morning, because of the ship in port and the hunting of fattened fall animals, Thaddeus's was thick with men. Dawn loitered in behind her mother, observing the fishermen and sailors and the beards that swayed as Petra passed them. Chairs creaked and Dawn saw that some were considering her too. They usually ate at Thaddeus's when the rooms upstairs weren't full. Petra somehow finagled her way around the chairs, her swan hat bobbing to an empty table with a cloth on it. Caribou and bear heads and fish looked from walls that once surrounded tables of drinking.

Soon Thaddeus chased them down. "Is it just you and Dawn, Petra?" he asked.

"Frances too," Dawn answered. Her mother was putting her grocery sack on an empty chair.

"Sit at this table then." He started moving dirty glasses and plates off of a smaller wood table nearby. With his quick eye, he poured coffee and examined the hat simultaneously.

"Thaddeus," Petra had to shout into the din. "If there was a law about hunting caribou this year, would you take down that caribou head from the wall?"

"There's not goin' to be such a law," Thaddeus said, swirling the coffee pot.

When Dawn looked away from the people ogling them as if they were game, she ogled too. Thaddeus was motioning two women through the thicket of men to the empty table, both of them dressed in scarves that had the sheen of snow in the Northern twilight. Even Mrs. Helsunk would have balked at seeing them. They were much better dressed than the

---

women at Thaddeus's and from their expressions, it was clear that they were keeping to themselves.

Catalogs could not depict the gleaming hues of their swaying pendants and the softness of their sausage-shaped mufflers. Their skirts didn't look hand-sewed; they looked like the drawn fashions of clothing for parlors. The women took a considerable minute to calm their clothing before they sat at the table with a cloth on it.

Their faces were powdered in pastels. The pearly color of their eyelids and the doll-pink of their cheeks contrasted with the sallow face of a girl who hung behind them. She had a mane of hair with waves that made Dawn think of seaweed, the front strands pulled back with glittering hairpins. This took the attention away from the girl's wan unsmiling face. Thaddeus's woman, in her plain daytime dress, ushered them all to the table.

The girl's hairpins were nothing fancy next to the hats of the two women with her. They didn't remove their hats when they sat down. One was so lopsided and velvety that it reminded Dawn of a rabbit with one ear. In its petal-like folds were pearls and flashing pins.

The other lady wore a black cloche hat that fit snugly like the swan bonnet did on Petra's head. But hers was ridged with silver fox fur, matching a foxtail muffler at her throat, and her hatpin had carbuncles on it. She turned to Petra and said in a shrill voice, "What a remarkable hat! Did the swan come from these parts? Is it a trophy?"

The other woman stared at it with a frozen smile.

"No. It was no feat to take this swan pelt," Petra replied. She actually moved her chair to talk; she might be mistaken for one of the ship-going group. Dawn knew that these perfumed women could only have appeared here from a ship in port.

"Look at the swans down underneath. The whole thing is swan!" the one with the fox muffler said to the lady with the pearls on her head. *Her* muffler was the pink of early raspberries.

That lady moved her chair around the table, saying, "I've seen a hat like that before." Then she remarked to Petra, "I'm told that numbers of swans land near this coast at migration time. Is that true?"

"Who told you that?" Petra inquired.

"Oh, ah, one of the ship's sailors heard it from a native, I think," she replied.

Petra's voice became husky with frustration. "I've hardly seen any swans in the last years. This hat was made from a swan that died of old age. It nested in this area for more than twenty years. It's as illegal to shoot swans here as it is in California."

The ladies looked at each other as Petra told them about Bustle. Then they inspected Petra's unadorned forest-green shirtwaist. But Dawn was thinking that her mother's face looked more like those drawn in catalogs. For one thing, the catalogs did not have pastel colors on the faces. And for another, her mother's face had firm cheek lines like the ladies in the drawings. The lady with the pearls in her hat had such pudgy cheeks that her eyes were small and sunken. The lady with the fox muffler had a little hump on her nose, making it look crooked.

The girl was sitting farthest from Dawn, and she squinted at the menu. She was wearing a splendid blue cloak with silver trimming. When she looked up at the bear head on the wall, she winced as if she had sipped some brine.

Then Frances was coming towards them in her best hat with its fringe of arctic hare. Chairs squeaked as men moved for her to pass. She was one of the few women outside of Toddy's who fit into clothing like the women in the catalog pictures, never looking lumpy or gaunt as many of the women in church did.

Frances sat down and stared at Thaddeus taking orders from the ladies beside them. Then she said, "You wouldn't believe what I just heard, Petra."

"What?" Petra had her eye on Thaddeus too.

"You'd better listen, Petra. Deputy Sheriff Shamison is drying this town without mercy. He busted into Jon's house, yes, Smokehouse Jon's, and put him in jail last night for liquor. My father was going to accompany Young Fen out to the inlet again today."

"Jon! He was supposed to be at the smokehouse today. The people from the ship are buying salmon."

"The deputy's got him drying in jail. I guess your husband is trying to get him out. The deputy's out somewhere on someone else's trail though and Sheriff Farefax is at the harbor because of a brawling dispute."

Dawn's coffee burnt her mouth. Dismayed, she could hardly believe that the deputy raided the quiet Aleut man who was never in brawls. Sheriff Farefax was often heard saying that there weren't enough jail cells for all the drinkers in town. She wondered if Kenny was there when Deputy Shamison took his father to jail. She wondered if he would come to school on Monday.

"The deputy picks on natives when it's least expected," Petra said. "Young Fen's not even on his way to the inlet, I s'pose." She gazed grimly at Thaddeus rushing with the breakfasts of the ship people.

Then they all observed Thaddeus until he noticed that they hadn't just come for his coffee.

~~~

Their breakfasts came as Petra was talking about the long day ahead. When she asked Thaddeus if he had seen Alex lately, Dawn heard a plaintive voice asking her a question.

"Would you tell me about that fish?"

It was the girl with the women from the ship.

"I could tell you about one like it," Dawn said. "My grandfather's skiff almost capsized from a King Salmon."

"Tell me near the fish," the girl urged.

Dawn walked behind her, looking closely at her silvery hairpins and ribbons. They were like hat decorations.

"It's a fifty-pound salmon," Dawn said when they reached the wall.

"I don't really care about the fish. I've been seasick and I don't want to eat." The girl's face was haggard.

"Do you eat ship's biscuits?" Dawn asked her.

"Those horrid things? Only sailors eat them. I'm so sick of reeking fish. I can't look at this fifty-pound thing. They must have caught something twice as big because we ate it on board for days. Then they have smoked salmon here for breakfast! Horrid!"

"There's flapjacks. This is a King Salmon," Dawn said again. She wasn't sure how to proceed in talking to this girl even if she was younger than her. "Look at the bear on the wall! Can you believe it eats berries? Its paws are this big." She gestured with two hands. "Where did your ship come from?"

"Seattle," said the girl. "What are those yellow berries on the flapjacks?"

"Cloudberries."

"What a name for such puny little things. You've never really seen fruit, I guess. It doesn't look like there was much of a gold rush up here, either. Why, in California, they eat platters of citrus fruit and grapes in parlors painted with gold." Her face went sour as she looked at the bear head. "We lived in California before my father built a house in Seattle."

"I've heard sailors talk about Los Angeles," Dawn remarked, sure that she wouldn't dislike traveling by ship so much. "They went there to get over the rickets. I never heard them talk about gold paint. Maybe it's fool's gold paint."

"How could they see those parlors? Oh, you can't know anything. And they're running out of things up here. My father said they might as well start sending ice ships down again and sell the glaciers. My goodness, your mother's wearing an old shirtwaist with that swan hat!"

Dawn wanted to answer that the girl's mother had as much paint on as a totem face but instead she said, "They're still mining up here. But not at the coast." She stalked away. She wanted to eat her breakfast even though they ate salmon five times a week at her house.

"No please. Don't go yet," the girl cried.

Dawn turned back to her.

"They'll make me eat. I'll get sick with these animal heads staring at me."

The girl's face was so ashen that Dawn pitied her. "Look at the caribou antlers," she said. "You'll probably feel better on your trip back to Seattle. I've heard the ocean is glass on the Pacific."

Then a singing gull-like call came to them. "Mary Gladys! Marigold!"

Dawn wanted to see the girl's mother come to her, hanging onto her hat. But Mary Gladys turned away from the voice to read the placard under the King Salmon.

"I think your mother's hat is lovely," she said, ignoring her mother and stroking her hair near the silver fastener. "I wish I could have gone with my father today. I had taken a fall on deck. And then I found out that he was renting horses." She swayed, looking up at the King Salmon.

"The boat was tossing, wasn't it?" Dawn said. Sometimes she wished she had been through an ordeal instead of just hearing about them. The only ordeal she could speak of lately was Mrs. Helsunk's parlor.

Oscar had been in plenty of storms on the water but he knew the weather would hold the day they went to the inlet.

"Oh, yes. Tossing and foam on deck. I got to the captain's cabin though. My father was just making plans to ride horses with a man from here. A man with a gold nugget." She scoffed, looking around at Thaddeus.

"A man from here? You mean you were in port when you fell on deck?"

"Oh, yes. We've been stuck in this harbor for more than two days now. We were supposed to be on our way to Anchorage today. My mother and I haven't felt well enough to come off the ship until this morning. The guide man stayed overnight on the ship. He sells furs and ivory to my father. He was telling ghost stories about a swan."

Puzzled, Dawn ignored another "Mary Gladys!" that screeched even more like a gull.

"A swan?"

"Its pelt was haunting his sister. My mother said he had a gold nugget but when I asked him about it, he said he left it at the house. He was afraid the pelt was bad luck. He knew the swan and it led him right to a grizzly. But he didn't know which side the swan was on because the grizzly almost killed him. My father says he's a sad sack even though he's not very old."

"Do you know his name?"

"His hair is black as an Indian's and his name is Russian. I could hardly pronounce it. My father, he used to trade with Russians. But my mother says he's a half-breed and a guide." The girl looked as though someone had offered her salmon when she wanted bacon. "My mother said he knows where there are swarms of swans."

Dawn stared at Mary Gladys. Wanting to be sure she had heard everything right, she stalled her with a question that her mother sometimes wondered about people. "What's your breed?" she asked.

With more disdain than before, Mary Gladys replied, "Why, I'm an American, that's what. When I wanted to go horse riding, that half-breed man said, 'This is not the Oregon territory.' My father said it sure wasn't. But then, my father said he might bring me a swan feather or two. And then we came here and saw your mother's hat!"

Dawn stepped nearer the salmon placard. "Do you mean they went riding after swans?"

"If that half-breed knows anything. My father goes hunting when he's in port, usually for mink or fox. They rode this morning."

"This morning?"

Mary Gladys craned her head and then she pushed past Dawn. "And I had to come out of a reeking ship cabin to a reeking restaurant in hillbilly territory."

Because of the way Mary Gladys said *territory*, Dawn shoved her aside so that she could tell her mother about Uncle Alex. "You should try some sockeye," she said because the boys at school said that.

Scrambling behind her, Mary Gladys sputtered at her table, "That girl is as wild as the waves up here. She almost pushed me onto this dirty floor. They're coarse, Mother." She slunk into her chair. "My stomach! I can't eat!"

TWENTY-EIGHT

While the fuss was going on at the next table, Frances was saying, "They've been talking of moving back to Manitoba in the spring. It's all I can do to remind my mother of the cold there."

When Dawn said, "Uncle Alex," Frances gave full attention to her whispering. "He's guiding ship people to the inlet! That girl told me. He's guiding her father."

With a quick look at Frances, Petra clutched at her hat ties. "I've had a feeling about Alex."

"He didn't even stop by your house," Frances said.

"He stayed overnight on the ship," Dawn said. Then she gulped her tepid coffee and saw Mary Gladys's mother unfastening the silver clasps on her splendid coat.

For all the restaurant to hear, Mary Gladys's mother said, "You couldn't go riding because they've gone to hunt bear, Mary Gladys! Please eat something now instead of talking."

After hearing about these hunting hopes, Petra stood up and neared the next table. "Are your men hunting with a man named Tuskoffey today?" She was undoing the ties to her swan hat and that held their attention.

"Is that how you say his name?" Mary Gladys's mother asked.

Her friend pulled her fluffy muffler as if to shield herself.

Dawn chewed her flapjacks nervously. Then she heard Mary Gladys say, "They're as coarse as sailors, Mother."

"Mary Gladys."

Petra demanded, "Where did they go this morning?"

Dawn heard chairs grinding nearby. Her mother turned to see that the men were listening. To gain the situation, Petra removed the swan hat and held it at the level of the women's heads.

"Our people don't know this territory very well," the woman in the raspberry muffler said. "That man Tuskoffey is their guide. They went to wherever there are bear and fox. The guide has some traps set."

"In this weather? That man Tuskoffey wouldn't take your men to the traps in the fog," Petra said. Loathing had come into her voice while the hat wafted in her hand.

"He said the fog would lift. And while everyone is sober, he keeps secrets about the U. S. territory like that gold nugget of his," the woman in the raspberry muffler sniffed.

Mary Gladys's mother, looking disgusted, turned away towards her daughter while Frances shifted her chair around. Petra, not seeing her, bumped the hat off of the chair back. It slipped from her hand and sailed to the floor like a dead animal.

The men were chuckling at this interruption in the female quarrel. Others began admiring the scene while Thaddeus was hurriedly making his way towards their tables.

Dawn jumped off her chair and retrieved the hat. "Let's go to the smokehouse." Her mother took the hat and then they grabbed their sacks and left their breakfasts. The rumbling of laughter was a frequent send-off at Toddy's.

"I wonder if we might help at the smokehouse today," Petra said.

When they got there, Dawn's father was buttoning his hide jacket, looking disgruntled. Across the room was Jon, checking on a rack of salmon.

"I was just going to the inlet," he said, looking quizzically at the hat hanging in Petra's hand. "You'd better go home and throw out the medicine bottle. Shamison's on a rampage." He nodded towards Jon.

"Ship people are hunting at the inlet!" Dawn warned him.

"How do you know that?"

Petra said, "From the women who came off the Seattle ship. They were at Toddy's."

Dawn spilled out, "A girl named Mary Gladys got to talking with me about the swan bonnet. She said her father was hunting where there are swarms of swans."

"The women said Alex was bringing the men to fox and bear," Petra said.

Young Fen mused on the hat, flecked now with the boot grit from Thaddeus's floor. Then he said, "If your brother took them, they're probably hunting now. I'm going to find Sheriff Farefax. If they kill swans, the only way to catch up with them is to wait at their ship."

"Alex might want to see those ship men caught," Petra said. "Maybe he expects someone on lookout. Men like them are his trouble. They don't really listen to him except they got him to talk about the swans somehow. And they talk him into things."

"I'd think Deputy Shamison would be lookin' for liquor from that ship," Young Fen said.

"He listens to them, not the locals. Why, you're happy enough to sell to them without inquiring much."

Although they were trudging the boardwalk, it made Dawn berserk, thinking about the swans at the inlet. Mary Gladys might never see their feathers but they might be killed just the same. And then she thought of her Uncle Alex being apprehended if he came to the harbor with the shipping men. She cried, "But they still might be killing swans out there!" Her parents seemed to have given up hope of stopping it. "How can we stay in town when they're doing that? They might be hunting bear first, to cover up. There might be time."

"With Alex, that bunch won't take more'n a swan each," her father said. "And if I stop that, we'll stop those people poaching. Your grandfather is keeping watch right now. I sure hope he doesn't have a medicine bottle about. The deputy was gonna help with the migration. And Frances's father is out at the bottleneck, near the traps. I talked to Minister Calvert, and he was askin' if he could help. He and Miss Banrath might ride out and post themselves."

Dawn was nonplussed.

"Shamison picks his times, doesn't he?" Petra remarked. "But how can you stop Alex from going to the ship with those men? They'll probably make him carry the pelts. Don't you want to stop him before Sheriff Farefax does?"

Dawn's father exploded, "Well, what are we going to do about him?"

"It's those ship men who want the swans. Alex doesn't often take them to the inlet for hunting," was Petra's stubborn reply.

"And Shamison doesn't usually raid the houses of men like me for liquor." Young Fen looked as if he was about to be defeated as he went into the jailhouse.

TWENTY-NINE

"Couldn't we ride out there?" Dawn implored her mother as they started for their house. "It might not be too late. If Uncle Alex sees tracks, he follows them. They might be hunting something else first. I know the trails out there."

Her mother didn't say much to this as they rushed on to collect the medicine bottle from the kitchen. But then she gave Dawn a pair of pants and she put hers on too. They slipped out to the barn where Petra sent the contents of the medicine bottle gurgling into the ground. Her words were as soft and uncertain as the fog that settled between the foothills beyond. "They say that Deputy Shamison hunts game when he's looking for people with liquor. That's why he's got to turn some people in. I want to see if I can prevent Alex from going to the ship."

She went to unlatch the barn door while Dawn pondered Davy's father, thought to have the conduct of his badge. She told Davy about the migration when her father didn't even trust his father. But that shouldn't have anything to do with the ship people and her Uncle Alex.

"The fog won't be bad on the higher trail," Dawn said. "Uncle Alex might have taken those people on the new trail."

Petra was saddling their two horses, Zirca and Lead Boy. "If they're hunting the woods like those women said."

"Then we'll see their tracks going to the bottleneck before the uphill," Dawn said. "They probably wouldn't take the steeper trail."

They were going to be vigilantes. They might stop swan poaching if Dawn could give Lead Boy a sense of urgency. She had to ride the portly old horse, bought from a portly old miner.

Before they rode out, Petra stuffed the swan bonnet in a burlap bag that she attached to Lead Boy's saddle. "Maybe it would be good luck to take this hat back where it came from," she said as she jumped onto their bronze nag, Zirca. "In the story, the swans wouldn't let the hunter be one of them. People can't be swans. The hat's already worked as a decoy."

Dawn clamped her heels into Lead Boy but, as he seemed reluctant about the fog, she dug her heels in again. Finally, her boots made an impression on his thick hide and they took the boundary trail out of town. Where Frances's father usually took a trail to the bottleneck, they didn't see any horse tracks. At least the laggard horse began a heavy trot. Then they were on the road to the inlet, nestled not only in mist but in mantles of pine and Sitka spruce.

Fog lapped over the land. The view was so bleary that Dawn couldn't see wagon ruts and heather-fringed boulders until they were near. The burlap bag strung onto Dawn's saddle kept sailing up and causing her to flinch. As Lead Boy accelerated to a quick canter, the light bundle floated beside her. Still, Dawn had to slap Lead Boy to get him to gallop across the plateau in order to keep up with her mother. She seemed farther ahead than she was because the mist made only an outline of Zirca.

Where the plateau began to recede into scrub, Dawn jounced beside her mother and said, "The trail splits pretty soon. Sometimes Wallop still takes the higher one."

The mist made blinders of their way but eventually, they found the new trail. Petra jumped down from Zirca.

"Horse hoofs," she said. "They look fresh. Maybe four sets. It's probably the ship party. They didn't take the trails to the bottleneck."

"If they're hunting down here, they're still far from the water. If they stayed on the trail, they might see someone." Dawn thought of Deputy Shamison or Minister Calvert. "Uncle Alex might have taken them roundabout. To his traps at the bottleneck. If they're hunting like those women said."

"He wouldn't take them to the traps until the fog lifts," Petra agreed. "If they kept on the trail to the bay, then they're likely hunting swan."

"There's plenty of hunting between here and the water. They might run into a bear."

"Those ship men might have an idea where they're going. From talking to people. It's like Alex to confuse their course."

Petra let Dawn go ahead with Lead Boy at his careful canter. Furze had grown over the wagon ruts on the old trail and sometimes it cut across rock. As it got higher though, the spruce woods became sparse and the mist became less dense. When Dawn looked from the foothill parapet though, the fog made a cloudy lake of the land below.

She hurtled her heels into Lead Boy's thick flanks until his mane ruffled around her. Without the fog blinders, they could glide the trail at a much better speed. The swan hat bobbing from the strings of the burlap bag made her shiver and slap at Lead Boy with her reins.

Then she saw how the fog settled over the lake end of the inlet, just as the path began its slope downward. Dawn could hear Zirca pounding behind her as the trees became more numerous. But since the mist might hide a grove of trees, she had to let Lead Boy slow down. They were nearing the place where old Wallop refused to take the hilly trail and instead trampled the more level one that wove through the trees.

Finding the intersection of the two trails, Dawn stopped Lead Boy and dismounted. Her mother was soon beside her, examining the trail.

"I don't see any hoof prints except this." Petra pointed at the tracks of one horse. "They must have gone through the woods. At least they didn't keep on the trail to the bay."

"They'll hit marsh on the overland. That looks fresh but it might have been from yesterday, maybe Pa or Frances's father."

"It's not hard for Alex to distract those men from their purpose. He might of scared them about traps near the bay. I don't believe he wants to take them swan hunting," her mother replied, getting up onto Zirca again.

They hastened on although the trail was again clotted with fog. With the swan hat bobbing up again and the land overwhelmed with mist, Dawn felt as if she were sleep riding. The trees lurched at her as if they were dream things. As a few trees became leafy in the colors of precious metals, Dawn knew they would soon gallop into her grandfather's yard. Her grandparents were expecting her father.

~~~

Dawn's skin turned to gooseflesh at the view near her grandparents' cottage. There might have been nine-and-fifty swans in the soft downy mist. The horses had ruffled up the nearer swans while silver silhouettes floated on the water that gleamed from the haze above. They seemed to melt into a wing of white on the north side of the water. Nearer, the swans glided and swerved as if they were phantoms.

Petra slowed her horse too, looking at the lake with awe. And then she jumped off Zirca and ran frantically to the cabin door, throwing herself at it in her urgency. Dawn watched the swans as they began swaying near the shore. Thinking how Bustle used to be the swan that came closest when they were feeding, she made sure the burlap bag was secure on Lead Boy.

The yard was mowed down by the migrators. Seed and corn were scattered up to the cabin door. There were stray feathers and tufts of down on the ground where the swans fed. If only they could herd the swans to the yard, they would be safe from hunters there.

They heard Grandma Glenda slogging around from the barn. "Petra! Dawn!" she exclaimed. "I was expecting Young Fen to watch for poachers!"

"That's why we're here," Petra said. "Is Fen Senior around?"

"He heard a shot on the north side of the lake and has gone to see about it," Glenda said. "Frances's father was going to the bottleneck where he usually hunts. He thinks poachers might come by boat. And Young Fen was going to take the shore from there."

"The north side!" Dawn cried. She gazed out where the swans stirred the fog.

Petra explained, "Ship men are out hunting. We found out at Toddy's."

"We saw their horse tracks," Dawn said. "And their tracks went down the new trail. They didn't go as far as the fork though. They must have gone overland. But how could they get around to the north side of the lake? They'd have to pass around your cabin!"

Looking along the shore and at the swans, Petra said, "Alex is guiding those ship men to the hunting. He doesn't take them onto your land. But they know about the swans."

Glenda grimaced. "I'm not surprised about Alex. He could have taken them through the foothills. But let's hope he stops them from hunting swan."

Dawn despaired, "I guess you might not have seen them in the fog."

"Fen's been patrolling the shore, on foot and in his boat. We've only seen Deputy Shamison checking on stills. But that was yesterday. When he saw the swans, he said he'd find time to help us. He said maybe Captain Helsunk would help. I hope the horse tracks were theirs. But where is Young Fen?"

"He's in town. Shamison put Jon in jail for liquor last night," Petra said. "Young Fen got him out and when we told him about the ship party, he went to find Sheriff Farefax so he'd waylay any poachers at the harbor."

Glenda had just filled a large basket with corn and sunflower seeds for the swans. "Fen left for the north side of the bay only a while ago. Let's start walking around the south side."

Petra said, "If we all keep talking and Alex hears us, that would stop them. I'd like to intercept him here." She untied the burlap bag from Lead Boy and then they hastened across the yard.

Liberally, Glenda strewed the banks with the feed, saying, "We'll just walk along the shore."

Dawn was already running ahead of them along the water's edge. The barricade of fog was beginning to lift. Now she could see swans moving languorously on the blue lake, their wings shimmering like mother-of-pearl. She might have thought she was seeing the luminous glow of the fog except that she could hear their reedy cries.

Her mother bounded ahead of her while behind, Glenda was showering the shore with handfuls of sunflower seeds. As they jogged around a turn of the lake, Dawn could see the swans paddling back onto the shore to feed.

THIRTY

They had to wade through reeds and clamber over boulders. Petra stayed ahead, jaunting on ground that might be bog.

"What do you have in the burlap bag, Petra?" Glenda puffed behind them.

"The swan bonnet," Petra said, taking the hat out of the bag. She gave the bag to Dawn and they both scooped up seed from Glenda's basket. Then they all threw seed on the shore as they cleared it.

"Keep talking but not too loud to scare the swans up," Petra called from a turn in the trail.

Dawn scaled along rocks behind her, and then she called out towards the swans, "Pinion! Over here!"

Her mother stood waiting on a plateau of moss where the white welts of fog were thinning. It didn't seem likely that anyone was concealed in the thickets of brambly raspberry and sunken spruce. "Alex!" she called out.

Glenda sang out too. "Lily! Minion! Bustle!" She acted as if she had no idea that any poachers might be about. "Oh, when they find this feed, it's a sight to see."

Though her ruffled brogue carried to Dawn, her voice was thin and it mingled with the low hoots of the swans. They mounted the mossy ridge, their voices blending with the din of the waves and the disturbed wings. She couldn't see her mother now.

Then the swans began rustling like wind, yards down the shore. Dawn heard gunshot muffled in with the noise. The swans were sweeping along the lake, one after another, and winging up into the air.

The gunshot must have come from beyond a slope and Dawn was racing towards it, trying not to stumble into the reeds. Her grandmother cried out behind her. Beyond the slope, after brambles and more spruce, boulders and more running, Dawn heard a voice, one that was familiar. "I'll signal when he goes to the horses. Fen O'Raine can't fly across the lake."

The brush was swishing near Dawn. It was her mother. "I found the tethered horses," she said and then she thrashed through the brush to the shore and flung the hat into the lake. It sailed up, making an arc while Petra yelled, "Helsunk!" Then a gun went off amidst the sound of splashing water.

It was Captain Helsunk's voice that Dawn heard, calling now, "A collapsed sail! It's Petra O'Raine."

Dawn and Glenda straggled through the clumps of spruce to see Captain Helsunk and a strange man in a dark deck slicker. But the lake was a more dismaying sight with swans rising, their wings whirring through the mist. They flew upward in a glistening mass and soon blended into the farther fog.

Petra bolted past the thick undergrowth of the declivity. Dawn followed until she could see Captain Helsunk's snowy head and how furtively he moved. Then she stood stock-still, watching the worst thing. Uncle Alex was stooping by the bank of the water where his husky, Naomis, dropped a dead swan.

"You'll be caught, Alex," Petra said, creeping nearer to him.

Branches were snapping behind Dawn, too loud to be Glenda. And beyond Uncle Alex, two men stood boldly. They put down their guns while Uncle Alex held his. When Dawn turned around, she saw a horse picking its way above the boulders, a horse carrying Deputy Shamison.

"Alex Tuskoffey!" the deputy shouted. "You've shot a swan."

The deputy's horse sidled around Glenda. She put her hand on a bundle tied to the horse, as if to steady herself.

"No, Deputy," Uncle Alex was protesting. "I didn't shoot this swan." He pushed Naomis away from him.

"A dead shot, that guide," said another man, coming up from the shore. His hair was the gleaming brown color of Mary Gladys's.

A man near Alex jeered, "A shot as sure as the Russian red of your shirt." He had the patchy unkempt appearance of sailors and he wore a sailor's double-buttoned jacket.

"Oh, go pick up your gun. This is your trophy. I didn't even shoot," Uncle Alex said to him. He looked at Petra and then he looked at Dawn.

"Two witnesses against one, Alex," Deputy Shamison said. His easy reply was almost as impudent as Davy's retorts. "I'm goin' to have to take you in," he went on, jumping down from his horse. He began to fold up the wings of the dead blood-stained swan.

Uncle Alex stood stubbornly with one arm over the other, the gun limp in his hand. He stared up at the cloud of swans beyond them. Then Naomis came paddling through the shore reeds. Something white swished in her mouth, only this time, it was the sopped swan hat. The husky dropped the hat at Uncle Alex's sealskin-booted feet.

Dawn cried out, "She'll bring anything to Uncle Alex! He didn't shoot the swan!"

The men ignored Dawn. But her mother strode past Deputy Shamison and took the hat from the dog. "I saw who shot the hat," she said. "Captain Helsunk mistook it for a swan."

"Stay out of the way," Deputy Shamison said, beginning to hoist up the dead swan. "Captain Helsunk came out here to patrol."

Petra persisted, "You just said Alex was waiting for his dog to bring the dead swan. The second shot was aimed at the hat."

"I heard something sneaking out from the trees," Captain Helsunk said. "Someone who had a swan, I thought, and tossed it like they were going to shoot another. Alex is quicker than me with a shotgun."

Glenda came up from behind them. With shaky ire, she said, "That hat saved a swan, Captain Helsunk."

"I saw that what was still living was what mattered," Petra said. "A bullet hit this hat."

"It looks like Deputy Shamison needs something to wrap that poached swan in," Glenda muttered.

"I'd like you women to go back to your cabin now," was Deputy Shamison's reply. His eyes glared dully, like granite.

But Glenda had already tromped to the deputy's horse where she rummaged with the blanket pack. Dawn followed her and then she saw more swan feathers. There was another swan carcass tied to the deputy's horse.

Glenda cried, "The law be tried! There's another poached swan here!"

"That's right, Glenda," Deputy Shamison said. "I heard a shot when I got here, over on the north side. When I got over there, I heard some rustling at the shore and found this dead swan, near hidden by a fallen tree. Thought I'd catch 'em trying to take the trail around to your cabin. Whoever it is knows this land pretty well if they can get 'round that terrain over there. If we get on back to the cabin, maybe we'll catch 'em. Did any more men come with you?"

He faced Uncle Alex while the ship men looked questioningly from one to the other. Then they all looked at Alex Tuskoffey.

The deputy declared, "Alex here usually goes hunting with Verne down at Snow Clothing. The store was closed when I went by today."

Glenda quickly retorted, "Verne's up at the neck of the inlet, where he traps on the south side. He was going to look for boats! In case a poacher came that way."

"Alex Tuskoffey lead us here," said the man with hair like Mary Gladys's. "Left us in the woods. He said he was going to check on a trap. There's nothing in his traps, I guess. One wild goose chase, if you pardon the saying."

Stubbornly, Uncle Alex said in a loud voice, "You went back to the trail when I went to the traps. Looks like you met Captain Helsunk somewhere. You made me follow your tracks. You were goin' swan hunting with a different guide. He knew there weren't any traps out here. You didn't get lost."

Deputy Shamison turned to Dawn and Grandma Glenda. "I thought I ordered you women back to your cabin. We might see a poacher there."

Uncle Alex's black moustache drooped lower than Dawn had ever seen him frown. "You're snakier than any animal I've ever seen, Deputy Shamison," he said.

"I'm pretty shocked at you, Alex. It's the first time I've caught you poaching swans." The deputy seemed to be mocking. "I guess it's your obstinate native blood."

"I'm pretty shocked at all of this too," said the merchant man. "I thought we were going to get some mink today. We were waiting for the fog to lift. Tuskoffey there said the hunting was good the other side of his traps. He said we'd be sure to get something from the traps. Our horses needed water, we waited so long. We didn't know that there weren't any traps. Didn't know Alex was after the swans."

"My uncle said there were traps to scare you. So you wouldn't go into the fog without him," Dawn said.

The other ship men stared at Dawn and then at her mother and her grandmother as if looks would prod them on their way. Even though Dawn doubted that a poacher would come around from the north side, she turned towards the cottage. Trudging, she heard one of the ship men say, "Deputy, we don't want to take the overland route. Your prisoner said he put traps out. And he guided our horses into mire. We need to get back to our ship."

"Follow my horse," Deputy Shamison said. "I'd still like to catch the one who shot the other swan."

~~~

Dawn didn't want to watch her uncle taken into custody but she glanced around anyway, lagging on the footpath. She saw the party on horses, the oblivious dog loping with them, and that Captain Helsunk's dog was there, sticking to his horse. The lake was in ripples. Panic-stricken swans were probably the white flecks near the mountains now. They were flying in the daylight.

"I wonder if they'll come back here," Glenda said.

There was a sound of trotting ahead of them. It was Grandpa Fen on Wallop. He halted, encountering Dawn's mother.

"Is that a poaching party?" he asked, peering through the trees. "I heard gunshot. I sure didn't round up anyone."

Dawn replied, "Grandpa, they're taking Uncle Alex in. He says he didn't shoot the swan they've got. He says a man he was guiding did."

"Deputy Shamison has another poached swan on his horse," Glenda said. "He said he found it on the north side but not the poacher. The party from the ship came overland from the wagon road. The deputy is asking about Verne because he hunts with Alex."

Huddling around Wallop, they all waited for the hunting party. It was easier for Dawn to watch a line of swans, wheeling now like a broken wing in the cleared sky above the valley.

"Deputy Shamison!" Grandpa Fen called.

The deputy swung his horse around and it stomped over to Grandpa Fen. Then the deputy's voice snorted above the animal. "Fen,

I've rounded up an obstinate poacher. Gotta take him in now. The witnesses have to get to their ship."

"C'mon off your horse a minute, Deputy. I went after a shot myself to the north side of the lake. There might be another poacher out here."

Petulantly, the deputy slid off his horse. He made a sign to Captain Helsunk and then said, "I know that, Fen. The poacher might be comin' this way, unless he's got a boat somewhere for crossing the inlet. I can't stop the hunting altogether. Might be some natives over there. It might of been you."

"Me! I'd have caught this party here before you did if I hadn't heard the shot. They've been trespassing! As for a boat over there, Verne was gonna be down at the bottleneck to notice anyone taking a boat into the bay."

Dawn tried to look at her Uncle Alex. She could hear him talking to the ship men about going up to Nome.

"Perfect fog for a boat today, Fen. And trespassing answers with a fine," Deputy Shamison said.

"A fine to pay you for catching them. Where were you this morning before you found this poached animal?" Grandpa Fen's salmon-gray jowls twitched.

"I came as soon as I heard about a hunting party coming out here," the deputy said, slouching at his horse. "I had just begun combin' the shore. To be frank with you, Fen, I didn't stop in because I have to suspect everyone. I know that Alex and Verne hunt over here."

"Just a minute!" Grandpa Fen stooped over the ground where the deputy left a heel mark in the damp dirt. "You'll know the other poacher by your own boot print, Deputy," he dared to say. "Those aren't native boot prints over there. The poacher has boots like yours. Those are the only tracks I saw."

Dawn stared at the deputy's boots, now sliding into his stirrups. They were rattlesnake boots that came on a ship. She didn't know of anyone else in town that had boots like Deputy Shamison's.

"You've got a nerve making any accusations about me, Fen. I had to get down on the ground to go after that poacher. Course my boot print is over there. Making accusations after your daughter-in-law has been flouting that hat around town! As if that nesting swan never met with a bullet. You've been causin' all the women in town to want such a Sunday hat. Alex here said you wanted to sell that particular swanskin." The deputy held his horse taut, waiting to see what Grandpa Fen would say.

"I did. So I did, Deputy," Grandpa Fen said. "I won't lie to you. That was an old, dying swan that would never have made another migration alive. But it's only your boot prints over on the north side. And mine are over there after yours."

Grandma Glenda was wiping flecks of mud off the swan hat with the sleeve of her wool jacket. She ventured a cheerless look at Dawn's mother. Grandpa Fen had not denied the bullet. And though he sounded forthright and somber, telling the deputy about Bustle, Dawn couldn't look at him now. She stared across the ground, at streaks of swan's down still in the yard.

Deputy Shamison said, "I don't exactly know what the law would say about an old swan that you judged to be dying, Fen." Then he gave his horse a jab with his rattlesnake boots.

"The swan that flew as a hat!" Captain Helsunk said, having come closer on his horse so that Dawn could see his eyes glitter. "It soared like an albatross. Did you ever hear about the guilt-ridden sailor that shot down an albatross?"

Petra answered him. "I think it's only me and my daughter here who haven't ever shot a swan."

The men began to ride away.

Grandpa Fen yelled after them, "Come by the road next time, Captain Helsunk. Your motorcar might make it through."

Dawn could only see her Uncle Alex, surrounded by the men from the States. The ends of his moustache seemed to have drooped lower than ever. He was what Mary Gladys had described him, a sad-looking man.

THIRTY-ONE

Grandpa Fen muttered after the departing Captain Helsunk, "Like to see that motorcar stuck."

"I don't know why Alex guides men like that," Petra lamented. "I wonder if he'll pay or sleep on his cot in jail."

Grandpa Fen said wearily, "Shamison will make it look right. There were horse tracks and that kind of boot print on the north side, not any natives on foot. And he's got a nerve, suspecting Verne or me. I don't trust him but I can't prove anything against him. Unless you want to go over with me and look for yourselves."

Petra replied, "Alex says that people with stills only have to toss a fox in Shamison's path and he'll go after it instead of the liquor. The law Alex has always known is survival. Those men sell in ports where liquor and swan pelts aren't illegal."

"Survival was on anybody's mind who came to Alaska after a climate like Ireland," Glenda comforted her. "I guess people thought the swans were surviving well enough then. There were four times the swans that you saw today."

"Five times," Grandpa Fen said. "There were more swans than men trading with gold in those days. There were swans enough for the King of England and all his lords and earls. A sight too much for an Irish fisherman."

For the first time, Dawn didn't want to stay for her grandfather's stories. The story that should be fresh in her grandfather's mind, the story of how Bustle became a swan pelt, hadn't happened exactly the way she heard it.

Her mother must have felt the same way because she loped on towards Zirca.

Grandma Glenda's voice fluttered behind them. "Don't forget this swan hat, Petra. It'll dry right back to its shape. Frances can fix the bullet hole."

"No. Keep it here," Petra said, her voice ruffled too.

Shambling after her mother, Dawn demanded, "What did you mean when you said it was only you and me who hadn't killed a swan?"

"She meant what was true, Dawn," Grandma Glenda said. "Those men were swan hunting. I shot a swan when we were hungry here, the spring of 1906. There were so many swans during harvest the autumn before that they ate everything we grew. Except the potatoes. Fen spent all his gold on the land here."

Dawn turned back to the swan hat in her grandmother's hands. She wanted her mother to take the sopping hat with them, her misfit mother who had never shot a swan.

"How could you lie about Bustle, Grandpa Fen?" Dawn burst out. "You're the same as those men, breaking the law! The same as what they're saying Uncle Alex is!" She stalked towards her grandmother. "I'll bring the swan hat home."

The yard might be in mist again for all Dawn could see her grandparents now. She turned away and ran into Lead Boy's flank. Then she felt her grandmother's arm circling hers and leading her.

"No, I'm not so different from Alex, Dawn," Grandpa Fen was saying. His brogue broke like lake waves in the trampled, feathered yard. "It was a dyin' swan. Her pelt would have been torn up by wolves or wolverine somewhere, and probably right here."

"I guess that in the territory of the heart, the law doesn't seem so clear-cut. Dawn," Grandma Glenda said. "I know that Bustle couldn't have flown away with the other swans this morning."

"I want you to keep the hat here," Petra said. "Something about it must have made me sleepwalk. I haven't done that for years."

"We'll keep it for a few weeks, and to show the bullet hole," Glenda said. "I can repair it. If it's haunting people, it'll haunt Grandpa Fen."

"Glenda and me will keep patrolling the shore. I don't suppose Glenda will see any other boot prints on the north shore except mine and the deputy's sort of boots."

"You know what the deputy will say," Petra said. "That the native boots don't leave a firm print. Especially in this weather. And Frances's father wears sealskin boots when it's wet. The deputy knows that."

"Well, me and Glenda will take the skiff over there anyway so Glenda can examine the boot prints. There should be prints other than mine near Shamison's," Grandpa Fen said. "Young Fen should be on his way. I don't s'pose I can accuse the deputy of trespassing if he comes sneakin' over here again."

"What if some more migrators stop in tonight?" Dawn was staring out at the lake where a few swans were now huddled on the north side. She wondered where Pinion and Minion were. At least no one had shot a cygnet. "If there's anyone else out here, we could still patrol. And if we don't see anyone, we can say so."

"Well, let's get some coffee and refresh ourselves," Glenda said.

It was quiet on their side of the bay but something was rustling along the shore. Dawn didn't want to leave now since there were still swans on the lake. The rustling became louder and then they saw a horse coming. It was Verne, Frances's father.

"I heard gunshot," he said. "I was watching for boats. Waiting for the fog to clear so I could check my traps."

"It was a ship party. Come overland," Grandpa Fen said and then he told Verne about the deputy's insinuations.

Verne surmised, "Alex might as well have taken them through the traps. I was expectin' to see him. He'd been to the shack sometime lately to put out his traps."

Frances's father was a large man, dressed in wool except for his sealskin boots. His expression was tentative like Frances's, bringing on another's utterance.

Glenda declared that the only boot prints Fen saw on the north side were the deputy's boots.

"I've seen him hunting out here enough times," Verne said.

"Did you see any boats?" Fen wondered. "The deputy seems to think that someone might have taken a boat to the north side."

"I only saw one. And that one might have kept any sailors from dropping in."

"Oh, and whose was that?" Glenda said.

"Why, it was Minister Calvert out with someone. They were sitting in the inlet when the fog cleared."

"He said he wanted to help," Glenda said. "And Miss Banrath offered too. I guess she wanted to see the swans. Minister Calvert likes to fish in the bottleneck."

Fen figured, "You know, if you're right about seeing them, Verne, then you couldn't have been in the woods on the north side."

Glenda mused, "I didn't think Miss Banrath wanted to encounter a bear. Let's go in for some coffee."

"I'll stay and watch," Dawn said. She was still holding the swan bonnet and when she went to sit on the stoop in front of the cabin, her mother sat with her. Far out on the lake, the swans were circling and glistening on the water. But there weren't more than a dozen of them.

THIRTY-TWO

Dawn didn't see her Uncle Alex before he left for Nome. He slept on a cot in jail. When Dawn's mother and Frances visited him there, he told them that he had spent many worse nights on a bobsled. Sheriff Farefax knew that so he was satisfied to collect a fine rather than keep Alex in a jail cell.

Sheriff Farefax wanted people to know that he was particular about poaching, making an example of Alex Tuskoffey. When Dawn protested that her Uncle Alex hadn't killed the swan, her father said there was only one man's word against another's. And according to Sheriff Farefax, somebody had to pay for the poached swans. There had been so much argument about the second swan that Sheriff Farefax couldn't arrest anyone for it.

Minister Calvert and Miss Banrath went to the sheriff and said that Frances's father had seen right. The minister heard that the inlet needed patrolling. He liked to fish almost as much as he liked preaching and he figured he could help by watching there. Miss Banrath said that they saw a man on a plateau of rock near the shore and he looked like Verne. They also saw a small boat with sailors in it. The minister steered his boat close enough to warn them against going into the bay.

Still, the deputy surmised that Verne might have used a boat that day and in the fog, it would be easy for him to cross over to the north side and back.

"We didn't see any boat come out of the bay," Minister Calvert said. But he and Miss Banrath stood by the deputy. "It was foggy early. And Miss Banrath had to get back to her correcting."

Frances's father just stood his ground while Frances told the deputy why the Snow Clothing store was unattended and how they discovered the ship people's plan to go out to the inlet.

She'd had a conversation with the ship women before she left Toddy's. The woman in the raspberry scarf said that there must be swan hats everywhere in their town. Alex had shown her a swan hat when she'd come off the ship for air. She admitted that this happened in the late evening and that Alex had acted as guide on the boardwalk after she had been to Captain Helsunk's. He showed her his gold nugget and a swan hat that he might sell to her. He'd been saying on the ship that there would be plenty of feathers coming into the General Store.

Frances knew the ship men had gotten Alex drunk. And they had known there might be a swan migration that week. Captain Helsunk had been watching for it. The ship men would have found their way to the inlet and done worse if Alex hadn't been with them, scaring them about traps. That was what Alex told her when she talked to him at the jailhouse.

Frances had waited at Snow Clothing, fixing up a package of wool hats that she might say she was delivering to the ship. She wanted to stop Alex if she saw the hunting party first. But as soon as they came into town, Deputy Shamison made her open up all the drawers at Snow Clothing because he suspected her father of poaching swan.

"I'll not be suspected in this town," Verne said. "Me and Alex have been trapping over there for years. Everyone knows we haven't been poaching swans. Next spring, I'm headin' back to Manitoba. My wife's been wanting that for years."

Sheriff Farefax was at the harbor when the fur merchants came back. They didn't even have a swan feather for Mary Gladys on them.

Mary Gladys was probably falling down on deck somewhere near Anchorage while Dawn went to school the following week. In the schoolyard, Davy told everyone about Uncle Alex as if he had been along with Deputy Shamison. When Dawn tried to tell what really happened, the school children didn't seem to believe her, all except for Oscar. He'd never liked the way that Mrs. Shamison treated his mother. Kenny might have believed her but he didn't come to school.

When Dawn visited her grandparents with her father, Grandpa Fen urged them to take the swan bonnet home with them. He said that Glenda left it about more days than she took to patch it. When he complained to Glenda that she had a fishing net to mend, she put the swan bonnet in a place where she could admire it. It was as bad as finding Glenda's new china for his morning coffee instead of a cup that could break. An object of that resplendence and delicacy wasn't of much use for Glenda or him when he was about his business. Which was fishing.

Even so, Young Fen and Petra decided to fix up a parlor that they preferred to call a sitting room. First, Young Fen moved Uncle Alex's cot, the snowshoes, the fishing nets, and the hunting gear to the barn.

In the new sitting room, Frances warned that she had something very irking to tell. She had been busy in her back room with a swan pelt. She finished a swan hat for Mrs. Shamison after Mrs. Shamison became the possessor of one poached swan. Mrs. Shamison had gone to dinner at Mrs. Helsunk's wearing her swan hat. Somehow, Mrs. Helsunk had come into possession of the second poached swan and now she wanted Frances to make another hat. They were going to tell people how the hats were from poached swans and that there weren't any swan pelts for sale in their town. They were also going to tell everyone how they caught the poacher and about his jail time and his fine.

Petra was wearing her snowshoe hare hat at church when Mrs. Helsunk came in, balancing a large swan hat on her head. That Sunday, they listened to Minister Calvert's sermon about temptation in the wilderness for the fifth time since summer.

In the spring, Dawn rode out to the inlet with her father to see the swan migration. Pinion and Minion returned to nest there and hosted a small flock of swans. They huddled together in the midst of the bay like an island of snow. After that, Grandma Glenda couldn't bring enough swan feathers to the ship merchants and the storekeeper.

It was that many months later that Uncle Alex came back. He slept on the polar bear rug in the sitting room because he said that people in town treated him like a reprobate. When Young Fen got into an argument with him about the ship people, Uncle Alex said there was an extra bedroom at Verne's.

"That's not for long," Young Fen said. "Unless you're talkin' about his shack."

Frances had decided that she wasn't going to Manitoba. Her saying that had kept her parents in Alaska these last few years, she confessed. She admitted in the sitting room that she had given up on Paul. Then, she visited the sitting room with Uncle Alex.

Uncle Alex announced, "You can tell Young Fen that I'm not going to sleep on his polar bear rug again." He blew on his coffee until it misted.

"I'm going to stay in my father's house here," Frances said.

"Frances and I are getting married," Alex said abruptly. Before Petra or Dawn could make a fuss, he said, "Remember that story I told you, Dawn? About the hunter and the white birds and how the hunter woke up without the polar bear covering? All he had was two feathers."

Minister Calvert married them and Frances wore the swan hat with her gown. Uncle Alex gave her a ring as stunning, traded from a White Russian for furs. After that, he stayed in town more although he still went north with the new bobsled he built, coming back with furs for the Snow Clothing store and for the merchants who came there to buy from him. He was on hand to tell newcomers about the cruel cold journeys he made.

In the years that followed, the swan numbers increased. At each migration, more swans gathered at the inlet. There were two and then three flocks of migrating swans, almost as many as Glenda remembered. Dawn hardly ever missed a migration, especially when she was old enough to call herself a vigilante. Of the swans, there were only a few relics and mementos in town as reminders - feathers for a new hat, a wall hanging with swan feathers sewn in her mother's native pattern, and a hat that was stored in a rooftop.

THE END

Katherine L. Holmes lives in Duluth, Minnesota. Besides writing, she likes finding used books for her internet bookstore and hiking. Her children's fantasy, The House in Windward Leaves, was a 2013 Finalist in both the Indie Excellence Book Awards and the Next Generation Indie Book Awards. Her other books are The Wide Awake Loons, published by Silver Knight Publishing, and Curiosity Killed the Sphinx and Other Stories, published by Hollywood Books International. More at: https://sites.google.com/site/katherinelholmesauthorprofile/

www.ingramcontent.com/pod-product-compliance
Lightning Source LLC
Chambersburg PA
CBHW022127170626
46808CB00002B/881